MIRAGE OF DEATH

Ordinary green-foliaged trees appeared to float above the ground. In front of them was a collection of about a dozen houses, alongside were the beings themselves.

Adam strode unhesitatingly towards them. He had almost reached them when the transformation came. The trees, the houses, and the weird white shapes suddenly collapsed, dissolving, melting into the ground. Without warning a brown sea lapped out, reaching towards Adam's feet. We saw him struggle to free himself. And then we heard him scream. . . .

DIMENSION A

L. P. DAVIES

A DELL BOOK

Published by
DELL PUBLISHING CO.,INC.
750 Third Avenue
New York, New York 10017
Copyright © 1969 by L. P. Davies
All rights reserved. For information, contact
Doubleday & Company, Inc.
Dell ® TM 681510, Dell Publishing Co., Inc.
Reprinted by arrangement with
Doubleday & Company, Inc.
New York, New York, 10017
Printed in the United States of America
First Dell printing—March 1972

DIMENSION
A

CHAPTER ONE

It took a certain amount of courage to knock on the white enameled door of Mr. Leming's ivory tower. The Director of the Institute of Biochemistry was an august personage reputedly unapproachable except by senior members of his staff, and I was the greenest of junior trainees. There was much the same sort of feeling I had sometimes had before entering my old headmaster's study. But I was eighteen now— a man by anyone's standards—my sheet was clean, and if Lee's letter was right the Director would be more concerned over what I had to tell him than incensed at my interruption.

So I knocked and went inside. This was the outer office, a place of metal filing cabinets and duplicating machines, a strong smell of antiseptic, and a desk from behind which an acid-faced female looked up to demand shortly, "Yes? What is it?"

"I would like to see Mr. Leming," I told her.

A young man with gingery fair hair and a narrow, serious-looking, small-featured face watched me through a window behind the desk. It was only when he moved as I did that I realised my nervousness had made a mirror look like a window and I was looking at myself.

"Have you an appointment?" asked the female.

"No," I confessed, adding quickly: "But it is very important."

Supercilious brows arched, she eyed my stained white coat. "Name and department?"

"Gerald Morton. Department D."

She wavered, pressed a button and spoke into a receiver.

"A Mr. Morton would like to see you, sir. He says it's very important."

The gruffly metallic voice sounded annoyed and impatient.

"What's that? Who?"

"Tell him it's concerning Professor Maver," I put in quickly before the female had a chance to reply. She relayed the message.

"John Maver?" echoed the voice with undertones of surprise. Then, "All right. Send him in."

Mr. Leming sat behind the largest and untidiest desk I had ever seen. He had a round, clean-looking face, a white military moustache and silver hair brushed immaculately back with sweeping wings over each large ear. He wore heavy, black-rimmed spectacles, and his white coat looked as if it had been tailored.

"Morton. Yes." He removed his glasses. "Have we met before?"

"No, sir." And, in case he got the idea I had been hiding away in the darkest corner of some obscure laboratory, "I've only been here a few months."

"Yes. And you want to see me about Professor Maver." He nodded impatiently to a chair. "Draw up and sit down, Morton. Well?"

Taking a deep breath, I drew Lee's letter from my pocket.

"I received this letter from a friend of mine, Lee Miller, this morning, sir."

He frowned heavy impatience. I was to learn as time went by that he never wasted time or words, and expected those he came in contact with to do the same.

"Lee is Professor Maver's nephew, sir," I explained hastily, and his face cleared.

"I see. Go on, Morton."

"Lee works in Norwich but spends his week-ends with his uncle at Haweford."

"Come to the point," said Mr. Leming testily.

I did. "Professor Maver and his assistant have disappeared, sir."

"Disappeared?" White eyebrows tried to meet silver hair. "What do you mean 'disappeared'?" He nodded towards the letter. "Is that what that's all about?"

"Yes, sir." I took the letter from its envelope, eight large sheets filled with Lee's ungainly scrawl, and handed it to him. He replaced his glasses to inspect it, shuddered, dropped the sheets on the desk, swept off the spectacles again and leaned back.

"Tell me," he said succinctly.

It was difficult to know where to start, or, having started, how to put it concisely enough to satisfy my listener.

"The Professor and his assistant"—I reached for the letter so that I could refresh my memory—"Adam Sokel, disappeared from their laboratory five weeks ago."

Mr. Leming's brows lifted again. "Five weeks?"

I found the paragraph that explained the delay. "The police were in charge at first; then the Special Branch took over. They asked Lee not to discuss the disappearances with anybody."

"Which explains why there has been nothing in the newspapers. I was wondering about that, Morton. Professor Maver is a well-known personality. So the Special Branch are interested . . ." He brooded silently for a few minutes. "Defection behind the Curtain?" He shook his head in answer to his own question. "No. Not John Maver. But that's obviously what they suspect. I don't like the sound of it . . . Go on, Morton."

I selected another page of the letter and read aloud from it:

"'Uncle John and Adam had been working in the lab all morning. It's a new building, some distance from the house. There's a telephone that Uncle John rigged up himself connecting it with the house. At midday Adam rang through for sandwiches. Mrs. Robson—she's the housekeeper—took them across. Everything was all right then. Later in the afternoon Adam came to the house to collect a length of rope which he took back to the lab. Mrs. Robson said he looked excited. At six o'clock she rang the lab to ask if they would be coming to the house for tea. There was no reply, so she went across herself. The door was locked and when she hammered on it there was no reply. Then she noticed a smell of burning. Thinking there had been some kind of accident she ran for help. The police cottage is only a few yards down the lane and luckily the constable was in. He came back with her, forced the door open, and found the lab empty.'"

I looked up. "Then Lee goes on to explain that there are no windows to the place, only the one door, and that had been locked from the inside."

Mr. Leming stroked his chin. "Maver's nephew. What kind of person is he?"

I had been expecting that. After the first reading of the letter my mind had travelled along the same road of doubt. I was as honest with my listener as I had been with myself.

"Very easy-going, sir. The life and soul of the party. The same age as I am—we knew each other at the university. He's training to become a commercial artist."

"The type of person who might indulge in an elaborate practical joke?"

"Yes, sir." I had to agree to that. "But both his parents are dead. His uncle is his only living relative. I know he thinks the world of him."

"I see." The other nodded pensively.

"When I first came to work here, sir, I mentioned to Lee who the Director was. He told his uncle, who said he knew you very well. Lee says here in his letter that despite the instructions given by the Special Branch man he felt he just couldn't sit back and not do anything about his uncle's disappearance. He says you are the only person he could think of to ask for help."

"That's reasonable. Yes. Does your friend mention at all what work his uncle was engaged upon?"

I shook my head. "No, sir. But there is something . . ." I leafed through the pages, found the appropriate paragraph, and read aloud again.

" 'I think Mr. Leming will know the nature of Uncle John's experiments. Tell him that this farm is the one from which the farmer vanished back in 1926. Apparently, he just flicked out of existence while crossing the yard. Uncle bought the place a few years back and built the lab on the exact spot on which the farmer did his vanishing act.' "

Mr. Leming gazed thoughtfully into the middle

distance. "And now it would appear history has repeated itself. Yes"—he seemed to be talking to himself rather than for my benefit—"I am well aware of the bee John Maver had in his bonnet." He came back. "Where did you say the place was, Morton?"

"Haweford Farm, Haweford. I've looked it up, sir. It's about ten miles the other side of Norwich."

He reached to press a button. "Miss Travers. I have to go away. Cancel all my appointments for the next three days. Arrange leave of absence for Mr. Morton. I'll give you fuller details later."

His finger still on the button, he looked at me.

"Do you have a car, Morton?"

On the pittance of a junior trainee? That was a laugh. "No, sir," I told him.

"And mine is out of commission. Miss Travers, look up the trains to—Haweford, you said, Morton?"

"It'll have to be Norwich, sir. Haweford doesn't run to a station."

He passed on the information and leaned back.

"You had better phone your friend to let him know we are on our way," he said.

"The farm doesn't have an outside line," I told him. "I'll have to send a telegram."

Lee was waiting for us outside the Norwich station. Standing in the sunshine by his battered car, jacketless, white shirt open at the neck, face sunburned, thick black hair untidy as always, he looked more like a gypsy than an embryo commercial artist. His spectacles had slid down his beak-like nose and he pushed them up into place before taking my hand. Worry showed through his smile.

"Welcome to the wilds of East Anglia," he greeted me.

I introduced him to Mr. Leming, who had sat silently engrossed in work during the train journey and who now, in pearl-grey suit and matching Homburg, looked anything but a big noise in the world of biochemistry.

"There is a marked family resemblance," Mr. Leming observed with ponderous joviality.

"Uncle John is Mother's brother," Lee said. "She used to say I took after him." And then, awkwardly: "It's very good of you to have come, sir."

"The least I could do, Miller. Your uncle is a very old friend of mine. I owe him more than one favour. If I can't do anything else, at least I can try to persuade authority that there can be no question of defection to the East."

"That's what they're thinking," Lee said bleakly, picking up Mr. Leming's smart grey suitcase and opening the car door.

I sat in the front with Lee. As the car lurched noisily away, Mr. Leming removed his hat and leaned forward so that his face was between us.

"Have there been any developments since your letter?" he wanted to know.

"No," Lee replied steadily.

"The assistant—what was his name?"

"Sokel. Adam Sokel."

"No relatives turned up wanting to know what has become of him?"

Lee shook his head. "He never spoke of having any relatives. Or friends."

" 'Sokel'—" The other tested the name. "Foreign, I would say. Mid-European. Could even be Russian. 'Adam'—" I felt his shrug. "Universal. You meet it everywhere. What kind of man was he?"

"Smallish in build. Swarthy complexion . . ." Lee furrowed his brows. "I can't remember his ever telling me what part of the world he came from. But then he never did have much to say. It was hard work having a conversation with him. He had an accent of sorts—guttural."

"How long had he been with your uncle?"

"A little over two years. He came first as a gardener, drifted to odd-jobbing, then graduated to helping in the lab."

We had left the outskirts of the town now and were out in the country, fields spreading flatly on either side, relieved by occasional farm buildings and clumps of wind-angled trees.

"Have you any idea what type of work your uncle was engaged upon?" asked Leming.

Lee nodded. "Yes," he said in a flat voice.

"Yet you made no direct mention of it in your letter to our young friend here."

Lee smiled faintly. "I was afraid that if I did he wouldn't feel like going to ask for your help, sir. He might have thought I was pulling a fast one. And I didn't want to write to you direct in case a secretary or someone opened the letter and read it first."

"Commendable precautions," Mr. Leming said dryly. "And did your uncle take you into his confidence as to the nature of any progress he might be making?"

"No, sir."

"A pity." Mr. Leming rested his solid chin on the back of my seat, a schoolboy attitude that was very much out of character. "I can well appreciate why you turned to me for help, Miller. I am pleased that you did. But you must realise that I am a humble biochemist, not a physicist. The small knowledge I have of electronics is purely basic, gleaned during the short time I was an associate of your uncle's."

"I do realise that, sir."

"Yes. Doubtless you have your own explanation as to what happened to your uncle and his assistant?"

"I have," Lee told him.

Mr. Leming turned to me, one eyebrow cocked quizzically, his large face only inches from mine.

"And you, Morton; can you suggest any explanation for the mysterious disappearances from within a windowless locked room?"

And that, of course, was something I had been puzzling over ever since receiving the letter. There was no answer.

"No, sir," I said.

"Then let me supply a few clues upon which you can attempt to erect a theory. On the afternoon of September 23, 1900, a farmer by the name of David Lang walked across one of the fields of his farm in the small town of Gallatin in Sumner County, Tennessee. Halfway across the field, in the presence of three witnesses, he vanished into thin air and was never seen again. You may have come across the details at one time or another, Morton. The incident has found its way into various collections of inexplicable happenings. That particular disappearance, only one of many, is in the forefront of my mind because it is an example Professor Maver was very fond of quoting. He set great store upon the testimonies of the three witnesses.

"Much the same sort of thing happened many years ago on the farm to which we are now bound. Another man—again a farmer, but that is pure coincidence—vanished into thin air. And five weeks ago, two more people disappeared from the same place. A final clue to add to the collection, Morton . . . Professor Maver once put forward a theory, the theory of simultaneous worlds. The idea is that an infinity of worlds exists in the same space as ours, although occupying different vibratory planes. There . . ."

He leaned back. I turned to stare incredulously, and he was smiling a little.

"Well?" he asked when I remained speechless. "Still no solution to suggest? Or is it that you have one, but it is so wildly incredible you are reluctant to voice it? Never be afraid to speak your mind, Morton. That is to delay progress. Never be afraid to announce findings based upon established facts, even if those findings are so incredible they can only give rise to derision. Professor Maver had no qualms. He spoke of his theory to many of his colleagues. He believed that our world was only one of an infinity of worlds existing in the same space. That immediately adjoining ours he called Dimension A."

The dry, matter-of-fact tone of his voice, his placid face, the calm, almost casual manner in which he spoke, helped me through the stunning shock of revelation. The implications were immediate and obvious. Professor Maver had been trying to find the doorway to an adjoining world.

Lee's uncle had bought the farm from which the farmer had vanished long ago. He built his laboratory upon the precise spot of disappearance because he believed the farmer must inadvertently have stumbled upon the doorway to Dimension A. And now it seemed that Lee's uncle and his assistant had also found that door, and gone through it. But to where? To what kind of place? My mind raced ahead. Would there be fields and trees there, just like these fields now? And people . . . Would people live there? What would they look like? I dragged myself away from this wild train of thought.

". . . not the first to put forward such a theory," Mr. Leming was saying conversationally. "Einstein propounded a similar one. But Maver took it a step further. He suggested that our world was in contact with Dimension A at certain static points. Under certain conditions those points of contact became manifest. Any thing or person who happens to be on the spot at the time would fall or be sucked through the dividing wall."

"He has a collection of papers and newspaper cut-tings," said Lee, intent upon overtaking a lumbering farm truck. "Including the one about the farmer in Tennessee. There are hundreds of them . . ."

"There are indeed many classic examples," Mr. Leming agreed. "The small boy who walked across the virgin snow of a farmyard to vanish—if I may be forgiven for employing an over-worked phrase—into thin air, his footprints in the snow ceasing abruptly. And we have to remember that in this country alone on an average day twenty-five people diappear and are never seen or heard of again. Maver believed that some of them, not all, had been drawn into Dimension A. It is obvious why he selected Haweford Farm as the site for his experiments. It is equally obvious that Miller believes those experiments were successful."

"They must have been," Lee said tonelessly.

"I am inclined to agree, but I must reserve final judgment until I have examined the laboratory and its contents for myself. And if I am able to satisfy myself . . ." He smiled briefly with little mirth. "We will have an explanation that can be offered neither to the police nor to the Special Branch."

The car rocked over a hump-backed bridge. Cottages clustered tightly in the hollow beyond. There were a few shops, I remember, a tavern with a colourful sign—a knight on horseback with lance at a dragon's throat (would there be animals in Dimension A?) and a church with a squat grey tower.

A short distance beyond the village, Lee slowed. Then he swung off the road between white-painted gates to draw up in front of a half-timbered, high-gabled house that was far removed from my own private picture of what a farmhouse should look like. But I was later to find that Professor Maver had had the old thatched roof removed and replaced with red tiles, and that two new wings had been added. In the old days, it seemed, the place had been little larger than a cottage.

We climbed out into the sunshine, Mr. Leming stretching, flexing his arms, and gazing about him with interest.

"The air," he said. "One can smell the salt of the sea. Or is that my imagination?"

Lee caught my eye, smiled fractionally, then pointed towards a low, flat-topped building that squatted rather than nestled, ungainly and out of place in its rural setting, in the deep shadow of a cluster of trees at the far end of quite a large cobbled yard.

"The lab," he explained tersely.

Made of grey concrete, it was an ugly, unornamented, windowless construction that reminded me of the pictures I had seen of the old war-time air-raid shelters. I think it was the stark contrast between its alien, efficient-looking ugliness and the surrounding greenery that gave the impression of something dangerous and menacing.

"Yes." Mr. Leming gave the place little more than a cursory glance, being more concerned with his inspection of the house. "All in good time, Miller. First things first. One can best devote one's concentration to a problem when one's creature comforts have first been satisfied."

Then he reached to lift his case from the car. Lee beat him to it and then led the way indoors. The housekeeper was a plump-cheeked country woman whose starched white apron never, during all the time I knew her, became creased or dirtied. For someone who lived in the country she was unusually retiring, never inquisitive, never perturbed, going about her work as if nothing unusual had happened. She took the small influx of guests in her stride. Bedrooms had been prepared—in a soft, pleasant burr she gave us directions—and a meal had been laid ready.

It was mainly a silent meal, Lee's polite attempt at conversation drying up in the face of Mr. Leming's complete preoccupation with the food. We finished eating about the same time.

Leaning back, napkin to moustache, Mr. Leming expressed satisfaction with the meal and praise for its preparation.

"Excellent, Miller. Your uncle has found himself a treasure. An estimable woman, the housekeeper. In the olden days, John—your uncle—and I often discussed the pros and cons of marriage. We both agreed, I recall, that we were cut out for bachelorhood. Marriage is not for dedicated scientists. The marital state makes for rigidity of routine."

He pushed his chair back.

"And now I would like to see the laboratory."

CHAPTER TWO

We left the house by a side door, passed through a trellis-work arch of some purple climbing flowers, and emerged into the late afternoon sunshine of the cobbled yard. Mr. Leming, it seemed, had decided upon a calm, leisurely approach to the problem at hand. In no hurry to get to the laboratory he strolled along slowly, gazing about him with interest as he had done upon his arrival, commenting upon a derelict pigsty, asking if the brick building behind had once been a stable, stooping to pinch at a greeny-yellow clump of pyrethrum that had taken root between the cobbles, lifting his fingers to his nose, and inhaling pleasurably. And gazing about him, he was the one who first saw the small, stoutish man wearing a soft hat and a belted fawn raincoat who was making his way up the drive.

"The Special Branch bloke!" Lee exclaimed with dismay.

Mr. Leming peered through his glasses. "The walk and the face seem familiar. Yes," he said as the man came nearer, "I have had dealings with him before. Barnett. A reasonable man, as I recall." He became brisk. "I will handle this, Miller."

He strode towards the raincoated man, and the two met, hesitated and shook hands.

"I didn't know he was still hanging about," Lee said with some bitterness. "Looks like he must have had someone watching the blasted place. Keeping his eyes open for Russians with snow on their boots . . . 'Defected behind the Iron Curtain.' He must be mad! Still"—he shrugged—"it has been done. I suppose they have to consider the possibility." He changed his tone. "Thanks for bringing your boss down, Gerald."

"He didn't need any persuading," I said.

"I feel better now he's here. Something solid—you know. A shoulder to lean on. I hope to God he can make some sense of that equipment in the lab." Lee gestured apologetically, the sun glinting on his glasses. "All this weird Dimension A stuff—I'm sorry it had to be sprung on you like that. I couldn't tell you about it before because Uncle John said it would be better if I didn't. He was afraid of it finding its way into the scarlet press. Not that he would have minded being laughed at—he never did—but he didn't want reporters hanging round." He grinned. "I must say I admired the way you took it in your stride back there in the car. You hardly batted an eyelid."

"It took me all my time. If it had been anyone but Leming I would have laughed in his face."

"I know. Science fiction stuff for the birds. A step or two beyond flying saucers. All the trimmings—the mad scientist on the deserted farm. Only Uncle John wasn't mad, and this place isn't all that deserted. It's

not too bad for me, I've been reared on it. The way
he used to explain things made it easier to understand. And on top of it all, there's that pile of cut-
tings. I mean, we know all these people vanish.
They've got to go somewhere. And Einstein came up
with the idea first. He was no fool. More things in
heaven and earth, Gerald . . . Only Dimension A, by
all accounts, is neither of those places."

He kicked at a loose stone. "I'm babbling. Not
making sense."

"You are," I tried to assure him.

The stone rattled across the cobbles. "One-way
tickets," he said, watching it. "Did Uncle John and
Adam only have one-way tickets?" He turned to look
towards where the two men had finished their conversation. The Special Branch man was making his
way back down the drive; Leming was returning in
our direction. "I hope to God he will be able to tell
me," Lee said feverently.

"So far so good," Mr. Leming observed as he
joined us. He radiated great self-satisfaction. "Barnett
was inclined to be annoyed that you had ignored his
instructions, Miller. I was able to make him understand that you couldn't be expected to sit back doing nothing. Your own words, as I recall. I informed
him, which is true enough, that I am here along with
my assistant in a purely scientific capacity. My repu-
tation being what it is, he accepted the explanation
without question. He didn't see fit to explain why he
is keeping the farm under observation. But that is
obvious. I went to some pains to impress upon him
that I have known Professor Maver for a very long
time and that there can be no question of defection.
Now"—he laid one large white hand in an almost
fatherly gesture on Lee's shoulder—"shall we take a
look at the laboratory?"

The narrow door was set deep in the concrete. Of

unpainted steel, rusted at the corners, it screeched on unoiled hinges when Lee pushed it open. He switched on a light before stepping aside for us to enter. Wooden packing cases, all empty by the looks of them, were stacked against two walls of the narrow, cheerless room. There was a pile of straw and wood shavings in one corner. Facing us, in the opposite corner, was another metal door. Lee opened it and reached inside to switch on more lights before drawing Leming's attention to the smashed lock. I fretted with impatience during his close examination.

"No question of the catch having dropped, Miller?" he asked finally.

"With no one in the lab, sir?" Lee shook his head. "No. Although the police say that is what must have happened."

"Seeking the only rational explanation," the older man said dryly. "I think I agree with you again, Miller."

He stepped over the threshold, and I followed Lee into the laboratory.

Immediately facing us were three contrivances—the first things I noticed—arranged in the shape of a triangle on the concrete floor, and set about four feet apart from each other. All three were identical, standing about a foot high. Each consisted of a metal cylinder topped with a white dome resembling a large inverted eggshell, from the top of which projected a thin silvery filament. The whole was mounted on a metal tripod that as far as I could see was firmly attached to the floor.

Cables snaked from the base of each device, leading to what appeared to be separate groups of equipment arranged on wooden benches that occupied two walls of the room. Against the near wall were three large generators—at least I was able to identify those—and what seemed to be the three accompanying transformers. Cables from these were slung along hooks fastened in the wall, looped along them roughly, leading to the three banks of apparatus. Each bank, I could see, had its own control panel, each alike in appearance, each filled with an incomprehensible array of dials and indicators. There was the peculiar, unmistakable tang of electricity, the same dry smell one gets from the back of a television set.

Stepping carefully over the cables, Mr. Leming made his way to the benches and pored intently over one of the panels. He rapped his thumb-nail on the glass face of a dial, fingered a switch, stooped to peer at the markings of some kind of sliding scale, nodded to himself and, still stooping, moved along to the next panel, which he subjected to the same close scrutiny.

"Notes," he said tersely without turning from his inspection of the third and last panel. "Did he keep notes?"

"I think he did, sir." Lee stepped across the cables towards the first panel. "I was never allowed in here, so I can't say for sure. Certainly, there were none in the house. But Mrs. Robson said that the police took away some pieces of charred paper from this bench. It looks as if there's been a fire in this section."

"I had already discovered that," Leming said dryly.

I went to stand at Lee's side. Now I could see where the surface of the wooden bench was charred, where some of the cables had been burned through, where heat had scorched the plastic panel.

Leming turned from his scrutiny of the last panel to go across to the triangle of devices. Kneeling, heedless of immaculate trousers, on the dusty floor, he touched them with an experimental finger, then lowered his head until his face almost touched the ground while he peered beneath each white dome in turn. Grunting, he came laboriously to his feet again, dusted off his knees, and then spared a few moments in examining the generators and transformers before returning to the equipment on the benches.

This time he pressed a switch. Behind me, one of the generators started to hum, softly at first; then the sound increased. A step along the bench, a second switch depressed, and another generator was brought into play. Another switch, and now all three were in action. The muted roar filling the room made the floor tremble under my feet.

I think I expected something to happen there and then. From Lee's expression, he probably felt the same. We watched Leming as he went unhurriedly about his inspection, moving from panel to panel, poring over dials. He seemed to be comparing readings, spending the greater part of his time over the charred front of the first bank of equipment. Finally, he went quickly back along the benches, flicking up switches. The generators died. Removing his spectacles, he turned to look at Lee.

"The first conclusion to be drawn," he said, "is an obvious one. This room is impregnable. Which means that your uncle and his assistant left by some other way than the door over there. We have to assume that they found another door, that to an adjoining dimension. At the moment, that other door is closed. Our first aim must be to open it again so that they may return.

"I did warn you, Miller, that I have no great knowledge of electronics. Fortunately, this mass of apparatus is not as complicated as it appears at first sight. Its purpose is simply to produce a complex magnetic field of varying intensity.

"Briefly, each of the three sections of equipment is

connected with one of those poles on the floor. Each panel controls the power fed to its respective pole. Each pole will, when activated, generate a magnetic field. The three fields will combine to form the complex pattern which must be the door. Can you follow that?"

Lee nodded. "Yes."

"Good. Now, the controls on two of the panels have been locked in one position. This means that we will only be concerned with the current controlled by the remaining panel. Unfortunately, it is this first section which has suffered damage. I am puzzled as how this damage was caused. Each panel incorporates a safety device, designed to cut out the current automatically when a certain level is reached. All three devices are in working order, yet the one on this first section appears to have failed in its purpose. Miller, is there a possibility that anything has been tampered with since your uncle's disappearance?"

"I don't think so, sir." Lee shook his head. "According to Mrs. Robson the only things that were touched were the pieces of charred paper, which the police took away."

"Good." Leming nodded approval. "So we can assume that the readings on two of the panels are as your uncle left them. We are now only concerned with the readings of the three dials on the damaged section. Let us try to reconstruct the events leading up to the disappearances. Maver and his assistant had been working here all day. There is only one stool. This could suggest that one of them was seated in front of the panel while the other was perhaps taking notes of the readings. Now, instead of going over to the house for a meal they phoned for sandwiches to be brought to them. Would that be a usual thing, Miller?"

Lee thought. "No, I think that was unusual."

"Which suggests that they had either found or were on the brink of finding the door." Leming turned to look at the wall telephone. "I assume that is still functional?"

"Yes, sir."

"Excellent. We will have need of it. Now, later in the day the assistant—what was his name?—Sokel went to the house for some rope. I see no sign of it here."

"It isn't here," Lee confirmed. "I looked. There are some things under one of the benches." He went over to the bench, kneeled, and dragged out several long strips of wood and lengths of wire. A hook had been tied with string to the end of one of the pieces of wood. Another had a small metal can attached.

"Made in a hurry," Leming commented, bending over the bundle. "You can guess what they were intended to be used for?"

"Probes," Lee said briefly.

"For reaching, for taking samples. And the haste with which they have obviously been made suggests that there was no time in which to make or obtain more efficient instruments. The door was there. they didn't know how long it would remain. There is nothing here to suggest that their probings produced tangible results. There is nothing here with which they could have tested the most important factor of all, the atmosphere beyond the door. And yet they went through, one of them an experienced scientist—"

"An accident," Lee suggested.

"Everything points to that. I feel positive that your uncle would never have gone through intentionally after so little preparation."

I felt it was time I added something to the discussion.

"Perhaps one of them went through with the rope

tied round his waist, sir. But something went wrong and the one left in the lab was pulled through as well."

"An explanation that does seem to fit the facts," Leming allowed. "One worth keeping in mind. I think we have learned all we can of the event itself." He went to stand by the first section. "Our first task will be to repair this. Not a big job, I feel. Then the real work will start. Tedious work." He beckoned, and we went to stand at his side.

"These two dials"—he pointed to them—"are fixed and can be ignored. We will be concerned with the other three. Trial and error. With no notes to guide us we will have no alternative but to work our way through all the countless permutations of these three readings until we stumble upon the correct grouping. It will be like trying to open a safe without knowing the combination."

Mr. Leming peered down at his immaculate grey suit.

"I will need overalls," he said. "And tools. Soldering iron, screwdrivers, pliers." He rubbed his hands together briskly. "The sooner we get started, the better."

CHAPTER THREE

And so Mr. Leming took charge of operations. A telegram was sent to the Institute to explain our absence. I don't know what reason he gave. Wearing stained brown overalls that had once belonged to Professor Maver's assistant, he set about repairing the damaged section.

Lee and I assisted in a tool-handing capacity. We started work the same afternoon of our arrival, a Tuesday. Lee demonstrated that the phone was functional by calling up Mrs. Robson to have a meal brought across. At midnight, Mr. Leming laid his tools aside and decided to call it a day. We walked together across the moonlit yard to the house.

Mrs. Robson had gone to bed but had left a meal laid ready for us. It was our second sit-down meal at the farm, and it was as silent as the first had been. I ate without knowing what I was eating. Tiredness was only partly the cause of my lack of concentration.

I was living in a dream. Yesterday—an age ago, it seemed—I had spent the day poring over petri dishes and their unwholesome-looking contents. At five o'clock I had left the Institute to catch my usual bus home. After tea I had gone for my usual stroll through the park, sitting for a while on my usual bench watching whiter than white ducks paddling and preening on the muddy verge of the pond. I had walked back through golden sunlight and lengthening shadows to my digs. Home, I called that small, top-floor room.

That was yesterday. A sane, ordinary day. Like the one before and the one before that.

And now—

My new bedroom had a wallpaper of pink rosebuds, a ceiling with low beams and a pleasant view of the drive and the lane beyond. The ugly laboratory building was at the other side of the house. But being out of sight didn't mean that it and what it represented could be put out of mind.

The gateway to another place . . . Part of me was prepared to believe in the existence of another dimension. The other part found the idea incredible, impossible, horrifying. Another world—perhaps an infinity of them, all occupying the same space as ours. While I was standing here, my hand on the window sill, with the solid, comfortable farmhouse furniture all around, perhaps another man was standing in this very same place, but in very different surroundings. Or maybe not a man, but a creature of some kind. Or perhaps—even more terrible—perhaps nothing at all. Emptiness. Limbo. Airless space. That was a possibility that Leming hadn't considered. Or if he had, perhaps for Lee's sake he had deliberately refrained from suggesting it.

Despite the warm night air I shivered, my scalp creeping, the hair bristling at the back of my neck. I tried not very successfully to thrust those thoughts aside. I climbed between sheets that were smooth and cool and smelled faintly of lavender.

Lee woke me next morning. It was, he informed me cheerfully enough, almost six o'clock. Mr. Leming, he added, was already at breakfast.

"Sleep well?" he inquired as some time later we went down the stairs together. "No nightmares? No bug-eyed monsters and little green men?"

"I slept well enough," I told him.

"I feel a damned sight happier now I know something constructive's being done," he said, opening the dining-room door. The room was empty; Mr. Leming must have wasted no time over his breakfast. "I like your boss, Gerald. He may be a big noise, but he's not stuck-up. You know. And he's not above getting himself all mucked up doing menial tasks like soldering. Ah—" He turned as Mrs. Robson, complete with morning smile and laden tray, appeared in the doorway. "I may be worried sick, but I can still eat."

Half an hour later we entered the laboratory, Leming acknowledging our arrival with a preoccupied nod. He was engrossed in the business of soldering a broken connection.

We were allowed time out for a knife-and-fork lunch. "No point in starving the inner man," Mr. Leming said. "The outer man works all the better, thinks all the more clearly for having a good solid meal inside."

About the middle of the afternoon he laid his tools aside for the last time, wiped his hands on an oily rag, expressed the opinion that everything should now be in order, and as proof of that, made a small ceremony of flicking up the three generator switches.

Then he bent to closely inspect the dials of the repaired section. He was able to make himself heard above the generator thrum without having to raise his voice.

"Yes," said he. "Everything seems to be in order."

"All systems go," Lee interpreted.

Leming lifted silver eyebrows and peered over the tops of his glasses. "Quite so," he agreed dryly. And then he proceeded to lay down the routine we were to follow.

He showed us first how to feed in the power and control it by watching the fluctuations of the three quivering needles and adjusting accordingly. He warned us to keep a close watch on a larger dial set some distance apart from the rest. If the needle of that dial was to slide into the red, we were to switch off immediately.

We were to work in shifts. Just like a factory. To save time, so that not a minute would be wasted. It could take days, weeks, even months. A twenty-four-hour day it was to be from now on. Three eight-hour shifts, Leming to take the first one so that we could watch him in action, get the hang of the routine. He would start now, at four. Lee would take over at midnight. I was to relieve him at eight the next morning.

Leming had thought of everything. A mirror propped in front of the operator on duty so that he could watch the triangle of poles on the floor without having to turn round. The magnetic field of the door might be invisible when it came, so a long piece of wood was laid on the floor across the triangle. We were to keep our eyes on that marker. If the part in the triangle was to vanish or become hazy, we would know the door had opened.

The routine we were to follow was simplicity itself. And boring—incredibly boring and monotonous.

Adjust control, wait for needles to settle, look in mirror, make a note of readings, start all over again. . . . The sort of thing that after the first few minutes one can do automatically while the mind is on something else.

Leming said impressively: "Now, this is important. If either of you happens to be on duty and something happens, no matter what—anything out of the ordinary—under no circumstances must you try to do anything about it. You must immediately phone me at the house."

And then, without removing his overalls, without even bothering to wash the grime from his hands, he drew up the stool, seated himself at the bench, made the first adjustment, noted the readings, and we were off.

Lee and I watched the sequence of movements for a while. Ten minutes were more than enough for us to get the hang of it. At first, each time a new adjustment was made I found my eyes turning to that triangle on the floor, my whole body tensing, a dentist's-waiting-room feeling of fearful anticipation gnawing at the pit of my stomach.

It was a feeling that gradually passed away. I even found myself yawning, but that could have been the effect of nervousness, not tiredness.

After twenty minutes or so, Leming turned to look back over his shoulder, asking crisply: "All right?"

Lee nodded, and we answered together: "Yes, sir." It was odd in a way how we kept on calling him "sir," even though he had asked us not to. Respect as well as courtesy, I suppose.

"Good," Leming said. "If you are both certain you know what to do, there is no point in your remaining here. You, Miller, had better get some sleep. Morton, get out and about. Get plenty of fresh air while you can. Don't forget that you will be sitting here for

eight hours at a stretch. A long time . . ." He cocked
an eyebrow at Lee, who answered the unspoken
question.

"At the back of this building, sir. No need to go
all the way to the house."

"Good." Leming turned back to the panel. Lee and
I walked across the yard.

"Sleep," said he, brown face turned to the cloudless sky, black hair stirred by the breeze. "At five in
the afternoon. What a thought."

"You'll have to try," I said tritely.

"I'll sleep if it kills me." He sounded as if he really
meant that. "I've no intention of dozing off during
my midnight stint. How do you feel about it, Gerald?"

"I'm getting used to it."

"No, not that. What do you think the chances are?"

"Your uncle found the door."

"That's what I keep telling myself. What's been
done once can be done again. But how long is it going to take?"

There was no answer to that.

Leaning against the trellis arch he plucked one of
the purple flowers. Clematis, would they be? I
should have known. My father was a gardener, and
I had been brought up with growing things.

"Going for a walk?" he asked.

"After tea," I told him.

That evening I didn't venture far afield but confined myself to an exploration of the spreading woods
beyond the farm. I'd always preferred the country to
the town, but then I'd been born and brought up in
a cottage on the outskirts of a Dorset village. My
parents still lived there.

I thought a lot about my home that evening. And,
reaching the edge of the woods, emerging on to the
road, I came across a cottage that was almost the

image of my own home. For a while, standing there, looking at the bright windows and neat curtains, the plume of smoke from the chimney, the scarlet geraniums in the white window-boxes, I was quite homesick.

It was tennish when I arrived back at the farm. Supper was laid ready for me. When I had finished, Mrs. Robson informed me placidly, she would clear away and then relay ready for when the other gentleman had finished work. If she was puzzled by this strange sequence of meals, she gave no sign. But then, being housekeeper to a scientist, she had probably learned to take anything in her stride.

And so my sscond day at Haweford came to a close. My first session in the laboratory started at eight o'clock the following morning. It was without doubt the longest eight hours of my life.

Leming dropped in about eleven. I thought at first that he had come to see how I was making out, but it seemed he had come with the idea of trying to improve upon Professor Maver's crude devices for testing the unknown. I altered the angle of the mirror a fraction so that I could see the triangle and his back at the same time. And after a while I asked him the same question Lee had earlier put to me.

"What are our chances, sir?"

"Chances?" He didn't look up from what he was doing.

"Of finding the door."

"We'll find it." He was busy with pliers. "The question is, how long? We don't know how long it took John. It could have been years . . ."

And now he seemed to be talking for his own benefit, thinking aloud.

"But much of that time could have been taken up in determining the fixed readings. I'm certain that to find the final readings he must have adopted the same hit-or-miss method I am employing now. Tedious but, so far as I can see, no alternative."

He came back to earth. "We'll open the door sooner or later, Morton. Nothing is more certain."

"And when we do, sir?"

"A bridge to cross when we come to it, Morton." He brooded for a while, his hands still. "We must devise some means of testing the atmosphere. I hope to God we find it breathable . . ." He shook his head. "Professor Maver is a very old and dear friend. . . ."

Wednesday slipped by, Thursday and Friday. The hours dragged slowly when I wasn't out walking or asleep. The house itself had nothing to offer in the way of entertainment, no television, not even a radio, and the only books were incomprehensible scientific tomes. I saw little of Lee—he was usually fast asleep when I came off duty at four.

And then came Saturday morning.

As usual, the sounds of the house coming to life woke me a little after six o'clock. Washing and shaving took me to half past, and that still left another hour before Mrs. Robson would have breakfast on the table. So, after passing the time of the day with her, not bothering to put on my jacket, I made my way through the early morning sunshine to see how Lee was faring after his long night. I remember stopping halfway across the yard while I wound my watch.

Lee, his shirt sleeves rolled up—the badly-ventilated laboratory was inclined to get warm—looked to see who it was, grinned briefly, and finished entering his latest readings.

"Tired?" I asked, for something to say.

He shifted on the stool. "More stiff than anything."

I wandered over to the generators. Heat rose in waves from their pulsating cowls. I looked at the triangle on the floor. They could almost have been three halved ostrich eggs, with wire protruding from the top of each. The magnetic field of the door would spring from those three silvery filaments. If ever the door came . . . And what would it look like? A solid prism of light reaching up to the ceiling, perhaps. Or maybe a kind of grey curtain. Or perhaps nothing at all, just the flicking out of existence of part of that piece of wood. A length of wood—such a crude, amateurish device to reveal the presence of a new dimension, the threshold of a new world.

And what would that new world look like? At the best, a place of trees and grass and flowers, of hills and towns and people. Of people like us. At the best . . . And the worst? Deep in thought, I stepped away from the generators without looking where I was putting my foot. It caught against the piece of wood, dislodging it from its position.

Lee swivelled on the stool to discover the cause of the noise.

"Clumsy clot," he said equably and swung back again.

I stooped to return the marker to its original position. One of the eggshells was perhaps two feet away from my face. Its filament was glowing brightly. And so—when I shifted my startled gaze—were the other two. I stared at them stupidly, wondering at first if I was imagining that incandescence, then suddenly realising its possible significance.

And what happened then happened so quickly that there was no more time for wondering. Before I had a chance to call to Lee, before I had a chance even to straighten from my stooping position, the glowing metal threads suddenly flared, fanning out into sheets of brilliance that met to form an unbroken screen. And at the same time something, some force, seemed to reach out towards me, gripping me with huge, invisible fingers, dragging me forward, towards the sheet of brilliance.

I think I must have shouted, perhaps screamed, for I had a momentary glimpse of Lee swinging round and coming to his feet, the stool flying. As I struggled desperately against the relentless sucking force, he came towards me. I saw his hands reaching out, I felt one of them clamp on my ankle, and then I was lurching forward, plunging through the dancing screen, pulling Lee with me.

CHAPTER FOUR

One moment I had been in the glaring brilliance of the laboratory; the next, I was in pitch blackness, falling into emptiness. There was the sickening, terrifying sensation of being in a lift that was plummeting down, out of control, into unimaginable depths. At the same time a hand seemed to reach inside me, grasping and twisting as if trying to turn me inside out.

I must have dropped for only the split part of a second, but it seemed to last an eternity. Then my heels struck something hard with a jerk that jarred my whole body. My knees buckled and I lurched forward, with no way of helping myself, hitting something solid with my elbow and then rolling sideways and downwards for a few more heart-stopping moments. Then I came up against some invisible obstruction that finally brought me to a halt, the impact driving the last gasp of air out of my lungs.

Stunned, I lay there—on some kind of slope, it seemed—in the darkness, only vaguely aware of a scuffle of movement towards one side. While I was fighting to regain my breath, I remember turning to look backwards and upwards in the direction in which I felt the door must lie. But there was nothing to be seen, nothing at all. And I remember too that I lifted my wrist to look at my watch, reading the message of its luminous dial. Why I should have wanted to look at the time, I don't know. Perhaps the gesture was automatic. Perhaps I was trying to find reassurance in something ordinary.

The breath returned to my lungs, sensation took over from numbness. I moved my legs tentatively but could not even make out their outlines, so black everywhere was. As far as I could tell I had suffered no damage.

I sat up, steadying myself on my hands—they felt as if they were resting on rock—and looked about me in all directions. I tried to pierce the intense darkness, hoping to find somewhere a break in it, a small gleam of light. But there was nothing—nothing to see, nothing to hear. Until the relief of Lee's voice, unsteady, coming from somewhere close.

"Gerald? Are you there?"

I nodded into the blackness. "I'm here." Then I moved my legs again, and my feet lost their grip and slid away. A rustling was Lee, moving in the direction of my voice. There was inexpressible comfort in the touch of his groping hand on my shoulder, in his sigh of relief, in his "So there you are. . . ."

I wondered if this strange new dimension was always like this, if we had fallen into a world of perpetual midnight. At least the air was breathable, and warm, perhaps even warmer than the laboratory we had just left.

And making that comparison brought home to me what had happened. It was my fault that we were here. When I saw the glowing filaments I should have reacted more quickly. Instead, with sluggish senses, I had just stared at them, the door had opened, I had been drawn through, and I had dragged Lee with me. There was some excuse in that I couldn't have known that the magnetic field would be so powerful, the force perhaps creating a vacuum that sucked everything towards it.

An apology would be so much wasted breath, but I tried to stammer one just the same. Lee's voice waved it aside.

"We found the door," he said. "That's the main thing. But by the look of it, the door has gone and shut itself again. At least, there's nothing to be seen back yonder. I think we can say it's closed."

He had an explanation to offer, and I was content to listen to the familiar tones of his voice.

"Overloaded. That'll be it. The opening has either switched itself off, or else blown itself out as it did when Uncle John came through. But this time things will be different. Leming's up there, and he'll know what has happened. He won't take long to sort things out. All we have to do is hang on here till the door reappears. And we may as well make the most of our time here."

Which was all very well—reassuring, certainly, for I had to agree with his assessment—but what could we do in a place where there was nothing to see, where it was too dark even to consider moving about? And how long would it take Leming to open the door? If that damned first section had blown itself out again, then he would first have to set about patching it up. And then would come the routine of dials and switches. And this time he would be working alone.

Digging my heels more deeply into the ground—grass, it felt like down there—to make sure I didn't start sliding down the slope, I looked about me again. My eyes must have accustomed themselves to the darkness. Far away to one side I could see light—I was sure of it—thin streaks of pearly-grey light.

Lee must have seen it too. "Dawn breaking?" his voice wondered. And then I heard the intake of breath of a yawn. "Boy, am I tired . . ." He discovered something else. "See, over there, Gerald." By the sound of his voice he had turned to look in the opposite direction to the streaks of luminescence. I turned. There, hanging in the darkness, far away, were two pale yellow globes about the same size as each other. It took me a moment to realise what they must be. We were beginning to learn about this new world. It had two moons, and if that was indeed dawn breaking above the opposite horizon, then night and day here didn't correspond with night and day on earth.

I heard Lee sniffing.

"The air's all right," he offered belatedly. "Fresh. That's something we can be thankful for. No scents borne on the breeze. Nothing to be heard either. Dead quiet. So where are we—out in the wilds somewhere? By the feel of it, I'd say we're on a steep hill. And that drop—" He grunted at the memory. "It certainly shook me up. How far did we travel before hitting ground?"

"It's hard to say." I watched the distant light get brighter. Then it was my turn to yawn. And quite suddenly, although I had been awakened from a sound sleep less than an hour earlier, I felt very tired. Could it be caused by reaction? I wondered.

"I reckon we must have fallen about five or six feet," Lee mused. "Which means the door—when we can see it again—must be hanging in the air.

The ground level here is that much lower than in the same place on earth. It's going to be a tricky job getting back through it again."

The light was steadily increasing. Now I could make out the pale oval of his face. And colours were tinting the sky—reds, blues, greens . . .

It was possible to make out something of our surroundings. The ground sloped away in front of us, steeply for a few yards, then levelled out to form a miniature plain, bordered with piles of tumbled broken rock. Backing the open space was a curtain of mist, motionless—but then, there was no breeze —that reached up to become part of the hazy sky. As the light grew, so the mist took on a weird greenish tinge.

All about us—we could see reasonably clearly now —stretching as far as the eye could reach, was a desolate, inhospitable landscape of red rock, interspersed with patches of sparse brown grass. Apart from the grass (and poor-looking stuff it was) the only living things seemed to be small, almost leafless shrubs that sprouted from crevices in the grotesque piles of rock. In the distance were one or two stunted trees or what, through the haze, might pass for trees, clusters of broad, palm-shaped leaves sprouting from the tops of very thick gnarled trunks.

"Alien landscape with a vengeance," Lee observed. "No little green men? It doesn't look very inviting."

"It could be worse," I said, remembering some of my past imaginings, and Leming's fears. "At least it's solid. And we can breathe."

He grinned. "And here we are talking about it just as if we'd gotten off the train at some village station and were taking our first look at some fresh part of rural England." He yawned again. "Damn! What's gotten into me?"

His yawn was more than infectious. I produced

two of my own in quick succession and then had to rub my eyes to clear my vision. And just for a moment I caught a whiff of some sort of smell, not the scent of growing things or the smell of soil warming under the sun, but a sickly sweet animal odour that was distinctly unpleasant and brought a small twinge of apprehension. When I tried to trace from which direction it was coming, it was no longer there. And neither, surprisingly, was the fear it had brought.

I looked at the curtain of mist, perhaps fifty yards away from where we sat on the slope. There was something about it, its stillness, the almost straight line of its base, the way it curved so evenly away on either side, the way it reached high into the sky, that suggested it wasn't a natural thing, not the product of warmth on moist earth. But I was too tired to think about it, too tired to draw Lee's attention to its strangeness. Weariness had taken hold of me, a comfortable, drifting weariness. There was no fear, not even concern at why I should feel so utterly tired after having just slept for over seven hours. I was completely relaxed and at ease.

Through narrowed lids I watched Lee lie back and close his eyes. I think he must have fallen asleep immediately. Without his voice and active presence I felt very alone. Uneasiness came then, and a return of reason. This sensation had to be unnatural. It was impossible for me to feel so tired otherwise. It was an effort now to keep my eyes open. Fighting leaden lids I was vaguely aware of the feeling of being watched by invisible eyes. The uneasiness grew. Then I was suddenly washed away in a warm tide of lassitude. I felt safe and secure. My drugged senses assured me that everything was all right, and nothing was going to happen. The door would open again; we would find Professor Maver and his assistant and take them back through to our own world. We would go back home again. . . . My home, a cottage set amidst trees, water sparkling, birds singing . . . I lay back, closed my eyes, and fell asleep to dream of the woods and fields of the countryside where I had been born.

There was no way of telling for how long I was asleep. I opened my eyes—not sure for a moment where I was—to find myself blinking at the mottled sunlight that filtered down through a tracery of branches and leaves. Then awareness returned, and memory. I sat up quickly, all tiredness gone, and stared about me, unable to believe the evidence of my own eyes. At my side Lee was doing the same, his face filled with incredulity as mine must have been. We had fallen asleep on a rocky, inhospitable slope in a desolate landscape that might have been on another planet. We had awakened to find ourselves in the green and gold of a very ordinary woodland glade.

Still on a slope, we were sitting on thick luxuriant grass of a brilliant emerald green. My first impression was of colour. All around were trees and bushes, banks of lush greenery dotted with the scarlets, blues, and yellows of flowers. In front of us a path opened invitingly between smooth brown trunks to meander away and melt into distant shadow. The sun was hot on our backs and a gentle breeze played on our faces.

Still looking about him, Lee pushed himself to his knees.

"I'm imagining all this—" His eyes rested on a bush of spiked purple flowers. "Lavender?" His gaze moved on. One hand moved through the grass. He looked down at it, tearing up some of the bright green leaves, holding them in his palm, then letting them drift back to the ground. "It's real enough . . ." And then he was angry. "What's going on? What's been happening?"

If I hadn't been so lost in my own incredulity and so startled, I would have found his anger comical. I think I did start to smile, but then, just for a moment, I caught or imagined I caught a whiff of that same cloying animal smell as before. And again I had the neck-tingling feeling of being watched by invisible eyes. I looked round quickly, fearfully. There was nothing to be seen but the flowers, the bushes, and the trees.

Lee had found an explanation for the transition. "Someone's been busy while we were asleep. We must have been moved bodily." He cocked an eyebrow at me. "I don't know about you, Gerald, but I didn't feel a thing."

"Neither did I," I replied. His assumption that someone or something had transported us here while we were unconscious seemed the only sensible answer. Until I came to move. Then I made a discovery. My heels were still resting in the hollows they had dug for themselves. And more than that: I had gone to sleep with my left hand resting on a small flat rock. The rock was still there, and round it the grass was still as sparse and wiry as it had been before—a circle of thin brown in lush green.

"We haven't been moved," I said in a voice I tried to keep steady and matter-of-fact. "We're still in the same place as before." And when he gaped at me, I showed him the proof.

"That's impossible!" On his feet, he gestured roughly. "All this? You're trying to say all this grew up while we were fast asleep?"

"We haven't moved," I said stubbornly.

He looked at the stone and the circle of brown. He moved across the glade to touch overhanging leaves. "They're real enough too." A thought struck him. "Just how long have we been asleep anyway?" He looked at his wrist-watch. "Ten past seven? No, surely not . . ." He held it to his ear and grimaced. "Stopped."

I looked at mine. That had stopped too, at quarter past seven. Probably damaged by the fall. But the glass was still intact, and the over-zealous shop assistant who had once talked me into buying a more expensive watch than had been my intention had assured me that among other things it was guaranteed shockproof. Practically unbreakable, had been the gist of his sales talk. Certainly, during all the years I had had it, this was the first time it had stopped.

Lee, a slim figure in white shirt and grey slacks, hair tousled, chin dark with embryo beard, spectacles as usual halfway down his nose, was making an exploratory tour of the little glade. Like myself, he had come through the door without a jacket.

"Rhododendrons," he discovered, and looked back over his shoulder. "In full flower. Aren't they autumn flowers? That's more your line than mine, Gerald. Maybe the seasons are different here, even if they have the same flowers. Primroses too . . . And they're out as well. I'm damn sure they're primroses, and they're supposed to come out in spring. That's something I do know."

Still exploring, he moved on. "Poppies. Buttercups. Plain ordinary buttercups and daisies. And that's an oak tree. See the acorns? Those are poplars. And the lavender—" He stooped over the cluster of purple spikes and then turned, puzzled in my direction. "But no smell at all. Not a whiff of lavender."

He came back to where I had struggled stiffly to my feet.

"I don't get it," he said worriedly. "It's all wrong. The whole set-up's wrong. First it isn't here, then it is. And now we might be in an ordinary everyday wood back home—just like the one behind the farm. At least at first sight . . . But the flowers aren't right, and the colours are far too bright. Like scenery on a stage, but not flat—three-dimensional."

I found something else that was wrong.

"Notice how quiet everywhere is, Lee. No insects humming, no birds. There's a breeze, but you can't hear the leaves rustling."

"I don't like it." He shook his head. "I think I'd rather have the rocks back again. And talking about that—before we fell asleep, when we were on that slope, I had the idea we were being watched. You know the feeling . . . It's the same now."

"Me too. I didn't say anything in case I was imagining it."

"It's not imagination. Neither is a rather nasty smell from time to time, like the lion house at the zoo on a hot day."

I nodded. "I noticed that too."

He frowned, pushed his glasses into place, and then shrugged resignedly.

"It's no use trying to make sense out of all this. I mean, we've got nothing to go on. This isn't our world. We're in another dimension where things are obviously very different." He grinned faintly. "Even if this part of it at least looks vaguely familiar."

"Different laws of nature," I suggested.

"Different laws of everything, I would say. We can't even start off by saying that all this stuff"—his gesture took in the glade—"grew from the soil the moment night had gone and the sun rose for a new day. It could be like that, but I don't think it is. The place has a different feeling . . . We'll just have to live from minute to minute, make the best of things and learn as we go along."

"And hope for the best," I said stupidly.

"As you say. And keep our eyes open. There's one thing I've noticed already. Whoever arranged for these trees to sprout out of nothing made a damned good job of it. It may be unintentional on the part of that certain mysterious someone or something, but they've arranged them so thickly together it would be impossible to force a way through them. And those at the back lie between us and the door."

He was right. Behind us the trees and bushes were packed so tightly together that they formed an impenetrable barrier. The only way out of the clearing was by the path.

A perfume of some kind wafted across the glade. Lee must have noticed it too, for he turned to trace it to its source. He looked up from a second close examination of the lavender bush.

"This is it, all right. No smell a few minutes ago; now it decides to reek to high heaven."

Somewhere in the distance a bird whistled an odd, off-beat melody like nothing I had heard before.

"And don't let anyone try to tell me that was a thrush," Lee remarked. "Or any other plain ordinary bird. Like everything else in this place there's something wrong with it. On the other hand, we could be the ones who are wrong. If you see what I mean. We're the aliens. Alien babes in the woods. So what do we do—venture further afield? We just can't stay here. Shall we see where that path leads to?"

It led to the unknown, and I didn't feel at all happy about what that unknown might turn out to be. There was something about all this artificiality that grated on my nerves and set my teeth on edge. And the persistent feeling of being watched didn't make things any better. I wondered absently if perhaps one of Lee's guesses wasn't right, that all this had grown up around us when the sun had risen, and that when darkness came again it would all melt away and we would find ourselves back on the rocky slope again. But that was an assumption we couldn't bank on. There was no point in just staying here and waiting for night to return to prove or disprove the theory. For one thing, there was no way of knowing how long daylight would last. For another, we would have to find food and drink. That was something Lee hadn't apparently thought about.

"The first thing to do," I said, "is to get organised."

Lee threw me a mock salute. "Yes, sir. For a start, we haven't the makings of a full-scale safari. Nor anywhere near it. I don't know about you, but I've only the clothes I stand up in." He patted his pockets. "Plus one dirty handkerchief and a comb that's missing most of its teeth. Oh, and a watch that doesn't go."

My contribution was much the same, only my handkerchief was clean and I didn't carry a comb. But checking possessions wasn't what I had in mind.

I pointed. "We know the door lies somewhere in that direction, somewhere behind the trees. I think we ought to mark this place in such a way we'll be able to recognise it again."

"The lad has brains." Lee looked about him. "No stones, so no cairn. Only the one your hand was resting on, and that's not enough." He looked at the place where I had been lying. "It would be a start, though."

But the stone had gone, and so had the circle of brown that had enclosed it. The rich green carpet extended unbroken across the glade.

"Someone," he observed a little shakily, "has done a pretty snappy repair job. And it's no use trying to guess who, how, and why. All right, so let's find some sticks we can drive into the greensward to mark the scene of the crime."

We parted bushes to peer into the undergrowth. I found nothing; neither did he.

"Not even dead leaves," he reported. "All neat and tidy as if a vacuum cleaner had been used."

We worked our way round the fringe of the glade with no success. Straightening, I reached to grasp one of the overhanging branches, intending to snap it off. As my fingers moved towards it, the branch moved away. Thinking the breeze had been the cause, I tried again. This time there could be no doubt at all that the branch had pulled itself away from my hand.

"More and more curious," Lee said, watching my efforts. "If I didn't know better I'd say that that tree —an ordinary oak by the look of it—is dead set against being touched. Let me try."

"Better not," I said.

He grinned. "Afraid it'll snap back at me?"

"How did it know I intended breaking a piece off?"

"I get it." He rubbed the side of his nose, dislodging his spectacles and then having to adjust them. "But trees can't see. And they can't read thoughts. Not usually, that is."

"These aren't ordinary trees."

"The hell with it!" he exclaimed, suddenly angry, and reached up to grasp the branch. And it stayed still and allowed his fingers to close round it. He tugged, there was a sharp crack, and he stepped back, holding the branch in front of him, looking at me over a plume of leaves.

"I know," he said wearily. "It doesn't make sense. Maybe I've got green fingers and you haven't. Or t'other way round. What're the odds, anyway."

He carried his trophy to the centre of the glade, there to force the broken end into the ground. It went in a few inches and then met resistance, toppling over when he took his hands away. He tried several other places with the same result. For all the rich, sappy appearance of the grass, it seemed to be nothing more than a thin carpet laid over solid rock. In disgust, he tossed the branch into the centre of the glade and left it there.

"That's the best I can do," he said. "Any more bright ideas before we hit the trail?"

"We're going to need food and water sooner or later," I said.

"Yes." He nodded without levity. "You're right, Gerald. Neither of us has had anything to eat since supper last night. And this sun's warm, very warm already. It's going to be hot later on. I'm thirsty now."

Just for a moment the feeling of invisible eyes boring into the back of my neck became very strong. I swung round but as usual there was nothing to be seen.

"Trees," Lee mused. "Any number of them, and a fair assortment. I wonder if it's likely there are any fruit trees among them?"

For some reason, perhaps because I had been thinking so much about the past these last few days, his words evoked a picture from my childhood. I was walking back home through the woods. At the old apple tree near the gate I stopped to pluck one of the fruits, taking it with me, polishing it on my sleeve, to the brook. Squatting on the grassy bank, one hand dabbling in the water, I sank my teeth into the sweet, juicy flesh. I came back to the present with the taste of apple in my mouth. The bird whistled again. And now there were other sounds—the gentle rustling of branches, and from somewhere not far away, the gurgling and bubbling of water.

"The place is waking up," Lee said. "You hear it?"

"Like the lavender," I said. "We talked about it

having no smell. Then someone gave it a smell. We remarked on the absence of birds. A bird started to whistle. You said you were thirsty, and now we can hear water."

"Very obliging of that someone," he said dryly. "All the same, I wish whoever it is would come out and show himself. Or herself." He cocked his eyebrow at me. "Or itself." He shook himself. "The hell with it! Let's go find where this path leads to."

So we set off along the path, always with that uncanny sensation of being watched. From time to time the bird gave its queer little trill of liquid notes, but we were never able to catch sight of it. The path curved between the trees. The sound of running water grew louder. We emerged unexpectedly into another glade, this one much larger than the one we had left. All around were the inevitable trees and bushes and flowers. And facing us, set in a nest of trees with a stream nearby, was, incredibly, a cottage.

I came to a halt, staring at it, refusing to believe what I saw.

"A refinement to the scene," Lee's voice said softly in my ear. "All very cosy. The finishing touch to the sylvan set-up." I felt rather than saw him turn to look at me. "What's the matter, Gerald? You look like you'd seen a ghost. You should be getting used to their tricks by now."

It was a few moments before I was able to control my thoughts, longer still before I was able to find my voice.

"This is different," I said with an effort. "The trees could be any old trees. But this isn't any old cottage. I know every brick of it. It's my home. That's where I was born. My parents still live there."

CHAPTER FIVE

The cottage nestled among the trees as if it had always been there. Ivy clung to one of the white walls, the ivy that as a boy I had used times without number to climb down from my bedroom window. The curtains at the windows were the pink and white chintz of my memory. The stream that sparkled at one side was my stream. There was the stone I had dragged to the side and heaved in with great effort to serve as a private stepping-stone. This was my home.

It was impossible. I tried to force my numbed thoughts into some semblance of reason. My home was outside a Dorset village. It couldn't be in two places at the same time. It couldn't have been picked up bodily, transported from our world to this and set down here for my benefit.

Lee voiced the only conclusion as it took shape in my mind.

"A reasonable copy?" he wondered.

"The spitting image," I told him, voice steady again.

"I figured it had to be by your face. A new effort on the part of our invisible friend or friends. Not like the woods—nothing to distinguish those. This is something purely personal. So how did they come by their building information?"

I was almost over my shock now. Just a copy . . . In a way, the lavender, the birds, and the rest of it all over again, but on a much larger scale. And with the added refinement that I had only thought about my cottage, not spoken of it. Which meant our invisible friends, as Lee had called them, had the ability of being able to read thoughts and lift pictures out of minds. And having done that, turn those pictures into solid reality, building something out of what—nothing? I offered this refinement for Lee's consideration. He had already seemingly worked it out for himself.

"It has to be," said he. "Another item to be added to the list. Extrasensory perception de luxe. From now on we'll have to watch our thoughts." He nodded towards the cottage. "Do we take a look inside?"

But that was something I was reluctant to do. I'm not sure why. Those were thoughts I didn't want to take shape. I think it was because I was afraid the people or things who lived in this weird dimension might, having made the cottage, have also gone on to make the people who lived there. That was something I preferred not to check on. Just because they had made a good job of the house didn't mean they could have made an equally good job of its occupants.

So I let Lee go on alone. He walked across the impossible grass, opened the gate, went up the path and knocked calmly on the door. He stepped back as people do, just as if we were back home, out for a stroll, and had decided to drop in on friends. A cold feeling inside me, I watched the door, wondering who or what might answer. Thankfully, I saw that it stayed closed. He knocked again, tried the handle, pushed the door open, peered inside, then turned to beckon me. I had to make myself go to join him.

The cottage was nothing but an empty shell. The brick walls were bare and unpapered. The floor was thick, spongy grass. There was no ceiling, no division of rooms, no fireplaces—for all there was a chimney outside—nothing except the windows and the curtains.

"Another piece of stage scenery," said Lee when we were out in the sunshine again. "Maybe they didn't have enough information to get cracking on the interior decorations. But they've made a damned good job of the outside. Bricks and mortar and timbered roof. This couldn't have grown up overnight. This has been made."

He examined the wall by the door, running his fingers over the brickwork.

"Looks like plain ordinary brick but isn't. Too soft for one thing. I can mark it with my nail. Looks like that sandstone rock that was scattered on the hillside. I'm guessing from the colour it's some kind of sandstone. So it's been made from local materials." He stepped back to look up at the roof. "Any more discrepancies?"

"Let's get out of here," I said.

He grinned at my voice. "Frightened, Gerald?"

I was, and there was no point in denying it. This, this copy of my home, had been the last straw. In nightmares the unseen horror that you know lurks round the corner is more frightening than the monster with which you come face to face. I was positive now that there was something invisible watching our every move, weighing up our reactions to the things it had made. There was the feeling of being a rat in a cage in some laboratory. I said as much to Lee.

"I don't mind admitting," he confessed, "that I felt a damned sight happier out there in the open. At least it was natural—if that's a word one can use in this damned place. A specimen in a lab, you say. I feel like we're in a waxworks with the proprietor trying to make up his mind whether or not to include us in his exhibits."

He stared at me as the notion took root.

"You don't suppose it could be like that, Gerald? Exhibits in their natural surroundings . . ." He shivered. "Let's get the hell out of here. Do we go on, or turn back?"

"Not much use going back. That's a dead end." I looked up at the sky, but the sun hadn't risen enough to show above the trees and so we couldn't use it as a guide. But there was a change to the sky. It was still cloudless, but the blue seemed to have darkened and now there were streaks of lurid purple laid across it. I drew Lee's attention to the change.

"Storm brewing?" he hazarded. "No clouds though. Unless that violet stuff passes for clouds." Then he rubbed the side of his face, and I found myself doing the same, not unconsciously copying him, but suddenly aware that the exposed flesh of my hands and face was tingling. The light breeze had died; the leaves hung motionless and heavy on the trees.

To leave the glade we had to cross the stream. Up until the moment we actually reached it neither of us had thought of the stream as being water. Thirsty as we both were, there had been other things on our minds. Now, using his handkerchief to wipe the sweat from his forehead, Lee stood on the grassy bank and looked longingly at the clear, sparkling water.

Something made me say, "No, Lee. Better not."

He crouched on his heels. "Looks all right." He touched it with a cautious finger, plunged his hand into it. "Feels like water."

"We can't be sure. Not in this place."

"I know what you mean. A fake like all the rest. It's one hell of a temptation for all that. I'd give anything for a drink."

"Only as a very last resort," I said.

"It's almost that now." He straightened reluctantly. "You're right, of course. We can't be too careful. Let's go before I weaken."

We used my stepping-stone to get across. Even its feel under my foot was familiar. I didn't look back as we left the glade, following the path which led back into the trees.

It was getting noticeably darker now, the purple streaks—when I glanced up at the sky—deepened, gathering and coiling ominously. The breeze that had previously died sprang up suddenly, but with a new, harsh feel to it, hot and tingling on bare flesh.

And after a while I began to have the impression that the many twists and turns of the path were leading us back in the direction from which we had come. With the return of the breeze, the weather was getting warmer. The light faded into a violet twilight, making it difficult to see for any distance ahead. Lee passed some comment about the tingling on his face and then frowned at the sky.

"Something nasty going on up there by the look of it," he diagnosed. "At least we'll have plenty of shelter if the rains come."

The warmth became an uncomfortable heat, a dry, prickling heat that was made all the worse by the ovenblast of the rising breeze. My clothes, sodden with sweat, dragged uncomfortably under the armpits. The tingling sensation increased, the feeling of a million needle-points being jabbed into exposed flesh. Rubbing only seemed to increase the discomfort. I tried covering my cheeks—the worst afflicted places —with my hands, but it made little difference.

We both heard the distant sound at the same time, stopping together in our tracks.

"Thunder?" Lee wondered, head cocked to one side.

But it was a steady roaring rather than an intermittent rumble. Overhead the branches were rocking violently, creaking with the rising wind, branches jostling angrily against each other. In the purple-tinged darkness we could barely make out each other's faces, even standing close together by the trunk of a tree where we had instinctively drawn for safety.

There was a strange moment of silence, and then the storm broke with startling, terrifying suddenness. But such a storm as I had never experienced before. There were no lightning flashes, no peals of thunder, no rain. Just the wind—a shrieking, howling inferno, a solid wave of searing heat that struck like a tornado, threatening to lift us off our feet and fling us away, and would have done so if I hadn't wrapped my arms tightly about the tree trunk. The pressure of Lee's body against my side told me he had done the same.

Our tree, massive and solid as it seemed, swayed alarmingly. The noise was deafening. My eyes closed tightly. I clung on grimly, desperately, the force of the wind driving my legs tight against the bark. A crash loud enough to be heard above the storm was presumably a tree brought smashing down. A series of smaller crashes marked its distant course. The very ground under my feet seemed to rock with the fury. Something—a broken branch it must have been— struck my shoulder and went hurtling on.

And then the solid trunk to which I was clinging

melted from my grasp so that I was left holding nothing. Immediately, the wind sent me staggering forward. I fell to the ground and crouched there on my
knees, my arms wrapped about my head to form
some sort of shield. Blinded and deafened, my body
as close to the shuddering ground as it would go,
with no way of telling what was happening, how Lee
was faring, I was alone with the storm. The wind, a
continuous, solid driving force, threatened each moment to drag me bodily from the ground and send
me sweeping before it.

Time had no meaning. Nothing existed save my
private world of darkness, unbearable noise and mis-
ery. An age passed. Then at long last the pressure
seemed to ease. The solid wind broke, becoming intermittent gusts. Slowly it abated, the din lessening.
There were longer breaks between each vicious gust.
Then it was over. I waited a few more minutes before raising myself a little, taking my arms from my
head, opening my eyes and looking round cautiously.
It was still too dark to see clearly, but I had the impression of being out in the open, no longer enclosed
within trees.

Gradually light returned. A few yards away Lee
was on his knees, looking about him as I was doing.
And we were back on the rocky slope where we had
first arrived. I recognised—with no great feeling of
surprise, for it seemed I had passed that stage now—
the desolation of tumbled red rock. The woods and
everything they had contained had vanished as if they
had never existed.

I pushed myself to my feet as Lee stumbled towards me. And it was clear that he too had lost the
capacity for further surprise.

"Change of scenery," he said. "Back to where we
started. Or rather where we started has come back
to us. I suppose if we stay in this damned place long

enough we'll get used to this sort of thing."

He used his handkerchief to wipe sweat-caked dust from his reddened face.

"And what do you think about that sample of local weather? I hope to God it isn't typical. I'm not sure I could survive another like that. My face feels like someone's been over it with emery paper."

My hands were painful too, stiff as if I had suffered an overdose of sunburn, but with a tingling sensation underlying the tension of the skin. There was a feeling of pins and needles when I came to flex my fingers.

I looked about me again, more carefully this time. It was certainly the same hill of our arrival in this dimension, but now we were on a different part of it. I could recall a certain grouping of the red rock, a rough pyramid with a spire to one side. Earlier, the pinnacle had been immediately behind the pyramid. Keeping my gaze on it, I made my way along the slope, the perspective slowly changing, until a spot was reached where, so far as I could judge, the landmark had resumed its original formation. I looked down and was pleased with the outcome of my little experiment. There, a little way down the slope, were the twin indentations where my heels had rested. I swung round then, hopefully, to look towards the summit of the hill. But it was bare, and so was the sky above it, a sky that was filled with the red haze of dust that was the aftermath of the storm.

Frowning, Lee had watched my manoeuvre; then his puzzled face cleared as he understood.

"A question of being thankful for small mercies," said he. "At least we know where the door is. And we have the means of marking the site. That's something we'd better do before the scenery decides to change itself again."

There was no shortage now of stones with which

to erect a cairn, although we had to search for those small enough to be moved. Collecting them, I was wary enough to keep a watchful eye on our surroundings—a precaution I was soon thankful for, because I noticed that my spire and pyramid landmark had suddenly vanished. For a moment I had the idea its disappearance might be the prelude to another change of scenery. Then I saw what had really happened. I let fall the stone I had been carrying.

"The mist," I called to Lee, "is on the move. And coming this way."

He straightened, turning to look for himself, absently flicking dust from the front of his now filthy shirt. "You sure?" He watched the mist. "Yes, so it is." And then he swayed, steadying himself with one hand against the cairn. "And I'm beginning to feel tired again."

I realised I was feeling the same. But not too tired, my mind not yet dulled enough to prevent me from linking the mist and the lassitude together. Something told me the two were connected, and the same something, instinct perhaps, warned me that danger lay behind that creeping wall of greenish vapour, that it was the product of some kind of intelligence.

Lee was having hard work to keep awake. But then he would be more susceptible to the emanations than I, for he hadn't a full night's sleep behind him. Fighting my own weariness I went to stand by him, gripping his shoulder tightly, shaking him until there was some reaction, until he opened his eyes to stare blankly at me. I urged him along the slope, guiding him between mounds or rock, choosing no direction in particular, my only aim to get as far away as possible from that insidious moving curtain.

When the ground levelled somewhat I changed course, moving away at an angle. As the distance between us and the mist increased, so the lassitude left me and Lee required less effort to keep him on the move. After a while, when I judged it safe—for the mist was now out of sight—I came to a halt, giving us both a chance to get our breath back. I looked about me, taking stock of these latest surroundings.

The dust haze which still persisted made it impossible to see for any great distance. All around, the weird landscape of grotesque rock-shapes, patchy brown turf, and occasional stunted palm-like trees reached away to become lost in the haze. Immediately ahead, silhouetted dimly against the sky, were the rounded summits of what could be either a nearby range of low hills or a more remote mountain chain. Under these conditions it was impossible to judge distances.

One of the small, leafless shrubs grew from a crevice at my side. I bent over it, dubious of the vicious-looking spines that projected from the contorted branches. They were easily capable of inflicting a nasty wound on any unwary hand or foot. I made a mental note to steer clear of them. One of the stunted trees grew nearby, and I went to study it more closely.

The trunk was an unwholesome grey in colour, and deeply indented, as if made up of a large number of thinner trunks welded together. From the top, about the level of my chest, protruded a tight mass of short succulent stems, looking for all the world like a bunch of peeled bananas. From these grew the large palm-shaped leaves, thick and green and glossy. The whole tree stood little more than six feet high.

The rest had given Lee time in which to recover. His inevitable grin was back as he asked, "Studying the local flora, Gerald?"

"What little of it there is." I nodded towards the spiny shrub. "I have the feeling we ought to give those a wide berth."

"I see what you mean." Then his grin turned to a

grimace. "Hardly the ideal site for a holiday camp. Rock and more rock. I suppose it must rain sometimes." He stubbed the tree trunk with his foot. "This looks like it needs a lot of water to keep thriving."

A fleshy-topped growth such as this did indeed give the impression of requiring a lot of water. That meant rain, and rain meant streams. Perhaps an over-optimistic chain of reasoning. In our world there are desert cacti that exist on little more than overnight dew. And this harsh landscape surrounding us now gave the appearance that rain had never fallen upon it at all. But there was water in this dimension. Or something that looked like water. That stream in the woods had seemed real enough.

"When you've finished your botanical studies," said Lee, "we'll press on. And I've no intention of being talked out of sampling the next stream we come across."

So we set off again, aiming towards the hills. For all the haze, the sun was oven-hot on our shoulders. Heat shimmered, mirage-fashion, over distant shapes. There was no path to follow; it seemed no one had ever come this way before.

After a while we began to climb. The slope was so gradual that it was hardly noticeable. The hills were closer and a change was coming to the scenery. The patches of grass were larger and greener. Trees were more plentiful; once we were forced to make a detour to avoid having to plough a way through a small plantation of them. And once a small furry brown animal, not unlike a rabbit from the little we saw of it, scuttled in front of us—the first sign of animal life we had so far seen.

The detour had resulted in a change of direction. Now we were skirting the lower slopes of the hills rather than heading directly up into them. We stopped to rest again in a miniature ravine with a steep escarpment on one side that afforded some shade from the merciless sun.

Lee lowered himself to the ground, cringed at its heat, leaned his back against the rocky wall and wiped his face with an already filthy and sodden handkerchief. His appearance gave me a rough idea of what I must look like myself. Dust and sweat had combined to mat his hair and streak his face. His once white shirt, now covered with red dust, was almost the same colour as his face. Even his spectacles were covered with a fine layer of red dust.

He took off one shoe, dragged off the sock, and moodily inspected a blistered heel.

"I suffer," said he. "And not a soul cares. Not a damn soul. And this is only the part you can see. My inside feels like it had withered up. The state of my mouth is nobody's business. I'd sell my soul—supposing there were any takers—for a long drink of ice-cold water."

"Quit moaning," I told him unsympathetically. I had never learned to know when to take him seriously and when not. I tried to forget my Saharan dew-reliant cacti. "It must rain here sometimes."

"Yeah." He massaged his heel.

A thought occurred to me. "That animal we saw . . . Surely animals of any kind, no matter where they live, have to have water."

"So that stream could have been the real thing." He replaced his sock and shoe. "And I let myself be talked out of it. Now we've got to find another stream. And something else too." One hand shielding his eyes from the sun, he peered up at me. "Or had you forgotten?"

Forgotten? Then I saw what he was driving at. I had forgotten. But God knows, I consoled myself, with all the things that had been piling up one on top of the other there was excuse enough. Maver and his assistant were somewhere in this dimension. If they were still alive. They could have wandered for days in search of water without finding any. Or they could have finished up in those damned artificial woods and come across the beings whose specialty was mind-reading and turning thoughts into pseudo-reality. Both ideas were equally disturbing.

"The way we are," I said helplessly, "there's little we can do other than to keep on going in the hope that we may stumble on something, maybe a clue."

"Nothing much we can do," he agreed, still shading his eyes while he squinted into the haze ahead. Then, "I was watching the way the heat shimmers. Like a mirage almost, you know? Pools and palms in the desert. Something to do with reflected and refracted light. You don't suppose those woods could have been some kind of mirage?"

"Mirages aren't solid."

"Not in our world. They may be different here. And that tree I was clinging to when the storm came didn't turn out to be very substantial."

I had been thinking earlier about that particular episode, remembering the uncanny sensation of something solid dissolving away in my grasp. But "dissolving" wasn't the right word. My impression now was that the tree had first dwindled in size and then collapsed, like a snowman shrinking in the sunshine, melting away to become a pool of water.

"I was using the same tree," I reminded him. "I know what you mean. But I thought we'd decided it was a waste of time guessing."

He lifted his narrow shoulders in a shrug.

"Just an inspired idea. And here's another—not that it'll do us any good. You realise that all this is existing in the same space as our happy little world? For all we know, where we're standing now might be a busy pavement with people bustling home to dinner. That's if it's dinner time back there. A bowl of fresh crisp salad, a couple of slices of cold meat, a jug of ice water—"

"And thou," I finished more sharply than I had intended. "Let's get moving again."

"So near and yet so far," he mused, coming to his feet. "I wish to God that Einstein had kept his blasted simultaneous worlds theory to his ruddy self." He managed a grin. "We've got to blame somebody, and Uncle John's presumably in the same pickle we are, with enough on his shoulders. All right, I'll lead the way."

And, because he was leading the way, Lee was the first one to notice a change of some significance. We emerged from a small ravine, crossed an open space towards a plantation of palms, and were on the point of changing direction to go round them when he stopped and pointed down at the ground.

There could be no doubt. We had come across a path. And, by the look of it, a well-trodden path at that.

My involuntary reaction was one of elation at this first sign of habitation. Then, as I wondered whose feet (and what sort) had levelled and hardened the ground, elation drained away and apprehension took its place.

Lee, I think, had gone through similar phases.

"What price Robinson Crusoe," he said quietly, wary eyes on the trees ahead. "And what price our little green men. This is a bit different from finding a footprint in the sand."

We went more cautiously after that. And by a cunning move on Lee's part—or it may have been unintentional—I found that I was now in the lead.

And so I was the first to see one of the occupants of Dimension A. I emerged carefully from a clump of palms to find myself on the fringe of another clearing, with another palm plantation behind. And something moved, disappearing too quickly into the shade of the distant trees for me to get more than a dim impression. But the shape was humanoid even though it seemed partially covered in brown fur.

Instinctively I dropped to my knees, dragging Lee down with me.

CHAPTER SIX

His dust-streaked features indignant, Lee was obviously on the point of voicing protest. I clamped my hand over his mouth just in time.

"I saw something," I whispered in explanation, and took my hand away to point. "Over there."

Our cover was two of the stunted palms that grew close together, their combined trunks giving adequate protection. I peered cautiously from my side while Lee did the same from his.

"You sure?" he whispered back. "I can't see anything."

"He was there."

"He?"

"It looked like a man," I said. "At least, about the same shape and size."

"What was it—" he started to ask. Then, at the far side of the clearing, leaves moved and parted and the figure reappeared, moving out into the open.

The brown fur resolved itself into some kind of animal-skin tunic, its brown colouring only a shade darker than the sun-tan of exposed face, arms, and legs. The shortsleeved tunic was tied about the waist with some kind of cord and reached to a few inches above the knees. Strips of the same fur were bound like odd-looking gaiters about the ankles. The feet appeared to be protected with sandals.

The man—it was a vast relief to be able to call him that—was short and stocky. A mass of thick, curly black hair reached low on the back of his neck. His eyebrows were heavily defined—the same colour and texture as his hair. His features were narrow and swarthy. A knife with a short gleaming blade was tucked into the cord at his waist. In one hand he carried what looked like a long thin bamboo cane with a small inflated leather bag at one end.

"Looks harmless enough," was Lee's whispered assessment. "Rural—oh, very rural. Back to the stone age, except for that knife. And what on earth's that contraption he's carrying?"

We found the answer almost immediately. The darkfaced man was working his way slowly along the fringe of the trees, his gaze intent upon the undergrowth. He stopped suddenly, freezing in his tracks, the bamboo tube coming up to waist level. There was a faint-sounding plop and something small and silvery lanced from the end of the tube. The man moved forward a few yards to pick up a furry brown body.

"So now we know," Lee interpreted softly. "Out hunting. Pop goes the weasel. I wonder if that little fellow is destined for the stew-pot?"

"What's more to the point," I said, "is just how lethal is that weapon of his?"

Lee squatted back, rubbing his chin. "I see what you mean. Effective on small stuff, anyway. Some sort of dart. You saw it?"

"I saw it."

The hunter, weapon tucked under his arm, the furry body dangling at his side, made his way back across the clearing. He paused to collect more of the dead animals from the grass before turning to disappear into the trees. It could be that, hunting over, he was headed for home. And home, I guessed hopefully, if it was as primitive as his appearance suggested, would almost certainly be near a river or stream. It was only then that I realised just how parched I was.

"He could lead us to water," I said. Lee was already coming to his feet. We crossed the clearing at a crouching jog-trot. That we could be going into danger was something I refused to think about. There was little room in my mind for any thought other than of the urgent need to find something to drink.

A path wound its way through the dark green shade of the small forest of palms. It was narrow, hemmed in closely by the trees, whose thick leaves met overhead to form an uncomfortably low ceiling that forced us to walk with our backs bent. That it was a much frequented path was clear from the way the grass had been worn away.

We saw no sign of our quarry until we reached the far side of the plantation. In the lead, I slowed down when the palms started to thin out, and straightened with relief. Ahead, the path cut across a small plateau towards what at first glance appeared to be an unbroken towering wall of red stone. But we were just in time to see the hunter vanish into a cleft so unobtrusive that without his unintentional help it would have escaped our notice.

We gave him a few seconds before following. The walls on either side of the cleft were high enough to completely exclude the sun, and we found the relief welcome. But it was only a short-lived respite. As we rounded a corner, the walls fell away abruptly, a new vista opening out. I pulled up so quickly that Lee bumped into me.

In front of us was a saucer-shaped valley, perhaps a mile across and encircled by low rolling hills. The fur-clad hunter was some distance away, walking briskly along the path that led gently down to a cluster of what had to be houses, set in a rough circle of stunted palms.

The houses were squat, solid-looking affairs, with sloping walls, flat roofs, windows, but no chimneys. They looked for all the world like four-sided pyramids that had been sliced across, the upper parts removed and roofs laid on top. And the roofs, as far as I could make out from the distance, were nothing more than thickish layers of dried palm leaves, a kind of browny-green thatch held in position with rows of stones.

There were about a score of them, all identical, each with a door made of rough pieces of wood, each with windows set in the same places. And the windows had glass in them, for I could see how they shone, reflecting the sunlight. It struck me as strange that in such a primitive settlement as this—each house simplicity itself, no pretence of gardens or dividing hedges, no roads, a village inhabited presumably by people who wore animal skin—that something so sophisticated and civilized as glass should have been used in the windows.

But there was no time to try to puzzle out incongruities. There were people moving about down there, all similar in appearance and dress to the huntsman, who had already joined them. Where there were people and houses there also would be food and water . . .

It was Lee who spotted the stream. He grabbed my shoulder and pointed with mute excitement to where water gushed from the rocks not a hundred yards away to go snaking, shimmering and sparkling, towards the rear of the settlement. But to reach the water would mean exposing ourselves. Licking parched lips, I leaned forward to inspect the lay of the land. There were rocks and piles of stones, but none of them were large enough to give cover.

"We've got to try," Lee said. "If we move slowly we might not be spotted. And if we are, for all we know the folk down there might turn out to be friendly. They look harmless enough."

They did—at least, apart from the blow-pipe weapons—but appearances can be very deceptive. But we were both in desperate need of water now, and the sight of it there was too strong a temptation to be denied. I looked down at the village again. Two fur-clothed men—I suppose they were men—carried a large basket between them. A little further away a group seemed engaged in conversation. Children wearing the same kind of clothes as the adults, only distinguishable by their size, played on the ground outside one of the houses. In its way, a pleasant, almost homely little scene.

"We'll have a stab at it," I said. "Take it dead steady." I glanced at his shirt then down at mine. There was little of their original whiteness left now to show up against the red background of the rocks.

Lee moved out of the cleft. Crouching, I followed, stepping sideways. My eyes were fixed on the settlement. No faces turned in our direction. Lee ran the last few yards to the stream to drop to his knees and plunge his face into it without any preliminaries, without bothering to test it. And I was equally incautious. I had never known anything so incredibly pleasurable as the feel of the ice-cold water on my face, of its sweetness as I gulped it down. And when the edge had been taken off my thirst I cupped my hands and scooped water, splashing it over my face and chest.

Still gasping, I squatted back on my heels and looked up. There, not a stone's throw away, coming purposefully towards us up the slope, were three of the fur-clad men, each carrying a bamboo weapon.

Lee saw them at the same time. We struggled to our feet together, turned, and found any chance of escape by the way we had come cut off by two more of the villagers, who had already reached the cleft. It seemed they had sharper eyes than we had given them credit for. We could only wait and see what they intended doing with us.

Lee shrugged and even grinned. "It was worth it, anyway," he said.

We became the centre of a small circle of unsmiling brown-faced men. One of them reached out to touch my shirt and then said something to his companions in a soft, sibilant tongue. That they made no attempt to talk to us told me that they must have realised, perhaps from our clothes, that we were strangers—at least to this part of their world. It was difficult to read the expressions on the flattish faces. If the men felt any surprise at finding us, they disguised it very well. For a few minutes they spoke together in their incomprehensible language, then the circle parted and one of them used his bamboo tube to point down in the general direction of the village, his meaning clear enough.

"Walk into our parlour." Lee shrugged again. "No option, Gerald."

So we started off down the slope. Our captors showed no violence towards us, no enmity, not even curiosity. The bamboos were carried loosely at their sides; no hands reached to touch the knives that were tucked into the cord belts. But the men were careful to hem us in for all that. One led the way, one walked on either side of us, and the remainder followed close at our heels. Escape, even if we had felt like it, would have been out of the question. For myself, I had a hearty respect for the simple but effective bamboos.

We were led through the centre of the village. The children broke off from their play, coming to their feet to watch us go by with silent, impassive faces. A woman—the first female of the species we had seen; slimmer legs, softer features, and longer hair being all that distinguished her from the menfolk— stood in one of the doorways, her unwinking gaze more intent upon our clothing than our faces.

The party came to a halt while our guards indulged in a second discussion, this time probably wondering what to do with us next. Meanwhile, one of them took hold of my wrist gently—the first time any one of them had touched us—lifting it to peer closely at my watch. I was afraid at first that he intended helping himself to it. Not that the watch was of any use now that it had stopped, but it was a kind of connection between this weird dimension and the stable, comfortable world we had left behind. But after a close scrutiny he left my wrist fall.

We set off again, this time guided towards one of the houses. The door was opened, it was made clear by gestures that we were to enter, the door closed behind us and we were on our own again.

There was much more to the interior than one might have guessed from the unprepossessing exterior. Certainly, there was no floor as such, only a hard-trodden mixture of earth and stone dust, but there were mats of plaited leaves to lend some small semblance of comfort. Stone walls, much thinner than the exterior ones, divided the place into rooms—oddly shaped rooms by reason of the sloping walls. The doors, held in place by thongs, were made of thick pieces of bark.

There were three rooms. The larger, into which the outer door opened, contained furniture of a kind—a

wooden bench, chairs, and a table, all very rough
and ready, but functional enough. At least the seats
were covered with layers of leaves in lieu of cushions.
The table had a smooth top, and there was even an
ornament on it—a vase made of glass, very clear and
sparkling glass, with no distortion on its smooth surface when I picked it up and held it to the light.

In the next room we found wooden bunks, padded
with more of the dried palm leaves. And Lee, exploring ahead, almost seeming to be enjoying himself, discovered the local version of a bathroom, exclaimed
aloud, called for me to come and see . . .

A bowl, attached to one wall, was made of glass.
So was the ewer, filled with water, that stood beneath
it, obviously there to make up for the absence of wa-
ter-pipes and taps. A very large bowl, oval in shape,
that stood on the ground in one corner, was certainly
a bath. Piled at the side were more dried leaves.

"Towels?" wondered Lee, touching them.

And there was even a mirror, a sheet of silvered
glass, attached to the wall above the smaller bowl.

"All the comforts of home," Lee remarked as we
returned to the large room. Seating himself, he looked
around. "No fireplace, though."

"Perhaps they don't need one. Tropical climate all
year."

"I was thinking about cooking arrangements."

"A sort of central kitchen," I hazarded. "The place
run on community ideas."

"Utopia." He grinned. "Without plumbing." Then
he became puzzled. "Why the sloping walls? Surely
they would find it easier to build them straight instead of at an angle?"

I went to stand at the window. Its glass was smooth
and crystal-clear without any tinge of colour. I ran
my nail across the mortar in which it was set, finding
it to be even harder than the surrounding sandstone.

"I wonder what they intend doing with us?" I asked.

"God knows." He didn't seem particularly concerned. "They've treated us decently so far."

I moved to one side of the window so that I could look towards the outside of the door. Arms folded, bamboo tube cradled against his chest, one of the dark-faced men leaned against the wall.

"Sentry on duty," I reported.

"Reasonable enough," Lee said placidly. "I noticed when we came in that there were no locks or bolts to the door, not even a latch or a handle." His gaze travelled round the room again. "No metal of any kind anywhere, Gerald. Had you noticed? No pottery either. Nor cloth of any kind. Only wood, stone, fur, leaves, and glass. All very primitive except for the glass. And toilet arrangements in the bargain. A stone-age cottage with some attempt at modern sanitation. What do you make of it?"

The glass was the odd man out. I picked up the vase again. When I rang it with my nail, it gave off a clear bell-like sound. It wouldn't have been out of place in a Mayfair drawing-room. On an impulse I flung it as hard as I could against the stone wall. I think I knew what would happen. It chipped stone but was itself undamaged, bouncing back to fall intact and unharmed to the ground.

"It looks like glass," I said, retrieving it.

"But obviously isn't. At least not glass as we know it. Those daggers they carry—the blades seem to be made of the same stuff. And they don't have beards, which means they shave. What with—glass razors?"

Coming to his feet, Lee joined me. I had returned to stand by the window.

"I'm not thirsty any more," he announced, "but I'm damned hungry. I wonder if they believe in feeding their guests?"

"I haven't eaten since last night either," I reminded him.

"Which doesn't make me feel any better." He looked down at himself, grimacing distaste. "What a ruddy sight. Who uses the bathroom first?"

"We can't toss for it," I said. "You go ahead."

While he was gone I climbed on the table and examined the ceiling. It was made, as I had guessed, of plaited dried palm leaves, thick layers of them lashed together with thin strips of the same material. We wouldn't need much effort to break a way through.

Some time later Lee returned looking strangely clean, shirt over one arm, announcing that he had used only half the water and that there was no soap. I pointed out our potential means of escape.

"It's an idea." Slipping his shirt on, he looked upwards. "Not in broad daylight though?"

"This house is on the fringe of the village," I told him from the door. "I noticed that when they were bringing us here. And there's a thickish patch of trees quite close."

Leaving him to mull the idea over, I went to the bathroom, where I stripped off my clothes and set about removing the grime that still remained after my dousing in the stream. There was little enough water, but I put what there was to good use. The leaves intended as towels performed their function better than one would have thought, but it was a case of dabbing rather than wiping dry. When I returned to the other room I found Lee seated contentedly at the table making great use of a glass spoon in a bowl of the same material that was filled with a white mushy substance. Another bowl and spoon waited for me.

"With the compliments of the management." He pointed with laden spoon. "Draw up a chair. Not much taste to the stuff, but it's filling."

It appeared that during my absence one of the village women had brought the food. There were even several small pieces of a kind of bread.

"She smiled," Lee commented. "The first time I've seen one of them smile. Did you notice that even the kiddies' faces were serious?" He mopped up the last of his mush with a piece of bread, popped it into his mouth, and leaned back. "That's better." Then he looked up at the ceiling. "Surely they must know we could get through there if we wanted to. Or maybe they aren't all that bright."

"They rounded us up efficiently enough," I replied, busy with my own food. Apart from a tang of salt the white mush was devoid of flavour. The bread, if it was bread, was equally tasteless. But it was, as Lee had discovered, very filling.

"The way we were," he said, "a gang of kids could have rounded us up. No, I was going by their expressions—vacant, disinterested. And look at the way they've set out their village—just a hotch-potch, no rhyme nor reason. And no imagination—all the houses built to look the same. And the way they behaved when they first saw us at close quarters. They didn't even seem curious. Think what would happen if a couple of them suddenly showed up in Piccadilly Circus. It would be a nine days' wonder. Milling crowds, cameras, headlines in the papers, the lot . . ."

"This isn't London," I said slowly. His words had set a new train of thought working.

"They don't look very intelligent," I said. "Even so, you would think they would have been startled to see us. Our faces are very different from theirs, our clothes, the way we talk . . ."

"I think I'm way ahead of you," Lee observed, "but go on."

"They weren't surprised because they had seen people like us before."

"And not so long ago at that." He nodded. "That's how I had it figured. Uncle John and Adam have been here for nearly six weeks. Long enough for these people to have become accustomed to the sight of them. And there's another thing. I haven't seen any kind of transport, not even animals that would serve instead of horses. In this place you couldn't get very far on foot. I'm guessing that Uncle John and Adam are here, in this very village."

"It's possible." I pushed my empty bowl away. "But if they are, and these types are friendly, you'd think they'd have taken us to them."

"Which could mean that they're either not here after all, or if they are, they're being kept—what's the word?—incommunicado. And in that case—"

Sweeping the bowls aside he climbed onto the table. As I joined him, the contraption creaked beneath our combined weight.

"We could use a couple of their glass knives," he grunted, tearing at the brittle leaves. A section came away, showering us with debris. Branches were entwined in the leaves, making it harder to wrench them apart than we had first imagined. Sunlight began to filter through.

I felt a twinge of remorse at the damage we were doing. A lot of work must have gone into making the roof. These people had treated us well enough, supplying us with what was perhaps all the comfort at their meagre disposal. We weren't even sure we were being held prisoners. But that was something we couldn't wait to find out. For all we knew, this might be only a temporary prison while something much more substantial was being prepared. I tried to assuage my conscience qualms with that thought.

The hole we had made was large enough for our purpose. Climbing up through it was easy enough, the low ceiling being only inches above our heads.

Lee wriggled through first, hoisting himself up, the ceiling sagging beneath his weight. Lying full length he reached down to help me up. For a few minutes we lay side by side in the sunlight, listening.

I raised my head cautiously. The palm trees, as I had earlier noted, were only a short distance away. In the opposite direction the sentry was out of sight, hidden by the edge of the roof. The open space in front of the house was deserted.

"All clear," I whispered to Lee's inquiring raised eyebrows, and we started to inch our way towards the edge of the roof nearest to the trees. The sloping wall was made for sliding down. Then we were running towards the cover of the trees. In the shade we paused to look back. Everywhere seemed quiet.

"So far, so good." Lee was still out of breath. He slapped one of the stumpy grey trunks with mock affection. "They have some use, after all. I wonder if they bear fruit." One of the huge glossy leaves swung against his face and he pushed it out of the way. "Something in the nature of coconuts, I would say. By the leaves, anyway . . ."

He had regained his breath but lost his smile. He puckered his forehead.

"What's the matter?" I asked.

"It just struck me . . . Talking of coconuts, thinking they'd be useful to flavour that porridge that they served up. When the woman brought the food in, I thanked her—automatically, you know. And that was when she smiled as if she guessed what I was saying, pointed to the bowls and said something in her own lingo. You know what? I think maybe she was telling me that they were only the first course, that there was more to come. The sweet, the pudding."

"Which means it won't be long before they find what's happened," I said with some bitterness. "A pity you didn't think of that before."

"I can't think of everything," he retorted resentfully. "We're only wasting time talking."

It was hard work forcing a way through the trees. The leaves, sprouting at face level, were the biggest nuisance. As before, it meant we had to move in a perpetual stoop. It was a relief to straighten when we emerged at the far side. In front the ground rose gently towards the rocky hills. We were exposed for the few moments it took us to reach a mound of jagged-edged red rock.

"I was thinking—" Lee started.

"Let's get further away first." I looked anxiously back at the village.

"There's a good chance Uncle John is in one of those houses."

"It's possible," I agreed.

He fingered his lip. "We managed to get away easily enough."

I saw then what he was driving at. "It wasn't all that easy."

"Granted, Uncle John is an old man. But Adam isn't. He could have done it."

"Perhaps they have escaped."

"Not through the roof, otherwise precautions would have been taken against the same thing happening again. I can't believe these people are that simple."

And that led to the idea that had taken root in my mind when we had been breaking out.

"The house could have been a temporary measure. They might be in some place that's more solid."

"Stone walls do a prison make. So long as the roof is of the same material. On the other hand, they might not be down there at all. But there's no point in moving on until we've made sure."

"We can't make sure in broad daylight," I said. "The best thing we can do is find some sort of hiding place in these hills—a cave, perhaps. Somewhere not too far away from the village and the stream. Then when darkness comes we can make a reconnaissance."

We left our cover, crossed an open slope, reached another pile of rock, waded through the stream that had been responsible for our capture, paused for another quick drink, and drinking, looked back.

Lee could have been right: there could have been a second course to the meal. Or maybe the woman had come back for the empty bowls. Whichever it was, our absence had been discovered and no time was wasted in launching a pursuit. A file of fur-clad men was emerging from the palms to fan out into a line before starting to climb the slopes. Some of them were armed with the familiar bamboo tubes. Others carried what could have been a larger version of the same weapon. They moved quickly, calling to each other as they climbed. Their voices, even from the distance, sounded angry. I had the feeling that this time they really meant business, that if they captured us again there would be nothing gentle about their handling of us.

CHAPTER SEVEN

That our pursuers had already spotted us was only too obvious from the way the line of men changed direction. They moved directly towards us as they climbed, their shouting more urgent. I guessed it was our shirts, filthy though they were, that must have given us away.

"Make for the cleft!" I gasped as we stumbled hurriedly along.

I thought we would have no trouble in finding the entrance to the narrow cleft along which the hunter had unwittingly led us to his village. It had been quite close to the stream. But the rock face was deeply indented, broken with jagged outcroppings, the many fissures deeply shadowed so that it was impossible to distinguish dead-end indentations from the cleft.

The going was getting harder. With no path to follow it was a question of struggling along the steep slope, making what use we could of the few handholds. Lee slipped and slid down a patch of loose scree. Precious moments were lost while I helped him scramble back up. A quick glance back showed that the gap between ourselves and the brown-faced pursuers had narrowed considerably. More sure-footed than we, more accustomed to the rough terrain, they were closing in on us fast.

And it was obvious now that we had missed the cleft. Panic came with that realisation. I fought it as I staggered on, telling myself that there had to be another way of getting through the towering rock face. My ankle caught in the trap of two flat boulders. More time was lost as Lee helped me free myself. We came to a narrow plateau covered with the small pieces of rock of some long-ago avalanche. There Lee stopped suddenly, one hand clamped to his side.

"Stitch—" he gasped. "Give me a second . . ."

My panic grew despite my efforts to control it. Staggering to the red-rock wall, I leaned against it, my heart pounding in my chest. Stooping to massage my bruised ankle, I looked back. The line had split. Now three men were coming up behind us, on the same level but still some distance away. Three more were moving immediately below, keeping parallel with us. The remainder were out of sight, hidden by a projection of the slope.

Lee, taking long deep breaths, swore, something I had never heard him do before. He took a few steps and had to stop. "No use." He looked about him. "If there was some way of stopping them, even delaying them . . . Stones?"

"No use," I jerked out. I had already thought of that. And the possible consequences.

He straightened, took another deep breath. "That's better."

I started off, but he had stooped to pick up a small boulder.

"No, Lee!" I cried sharply. "They've got weapons. They'll retaliate."

"Popguns," he grunted, weighing the stone in his hands.

"We don't know what they can do with them. And they've got another sort of weapon too."

The fur-clad men had been closing in while we were talking. I went to grip Lee's shoulder, swung him round angrily, knocked the stone out of his hands, even pushed him along. For a moment I thought he was going to hit me. Instead he set off across the plateau. At the end the slope steepened suddenly, affording no footholds at all.

Panic exploded sickeningly inside me again. My face streaming with sweat, I looked about, desperately searching for some means of escape from the trap into which we had stumbled. Immediately above us was another ledge, one that appeared to extend for quite a distance. By standing on my toes I could just get my fingers over the edge. Lee, without a word being spoken, used his shoulder to boost me up. I clawed my way, oblivious of a split knuckle and a broken fingernail, to the new level. Kneeling, I reached down to help him. He gripped my hand with one of his and used the other to grasp what seemed a solidly anchored projection.

But it was loose, shifted with his weight, rocked and then slipped away, leaving all of Lee's weight swinging on my arm. With an effort I managed to haul him up. We collapsed together on the ground. And the dislodged boulder went rolling and bouncing away down the slope, collecting smaller stones on its way, the miniature avalanche hurtling towards the trio of men below. Shouting, they scattered, but not in time. A flying rock caught one of them on the shoulder, sending him sprawling.

Lee, scrambling to his knees, showed white teeth

in a mirthless grin. "That's what I had in mind before."

Stupid though it was at such a time, I still tried to offer some sort of apology.

"Down there—I'm sorry for what happened, Lee."

"No." He punched my shoulder lightly. "Save your breath. You were right. It's just that I wanted to hit back at them. Now I have. . . ."

There was a temporary halt to the pursuit. Lee's unintentional victim was sitting up, one hand to his shoulder, his two companions bending anxiously over him. The three that had been following us on the same level had stopped in their tracks. And down below, the remainder of the party had emerged into view, coming to cluster about the injured man. From their attitude as they looked up at us, some of them pointing, I got the impression that they thought the avalanche had been intentional. And that, I felt sure, would bring retaliation. I was right.

Still crouching on my knees, getting my strength back to move off again, I threw another quick glance sideways. It was fortunate I did. One of the bamboo weapons was raised and pointed in our direction. I dragged Lee down just in time. Silver flashed low over our heads, and something struck the rock behind and tinkled to the ground—so close that Lee was able to reach to pick up the dart, holding it gingerly for our inspection. And with the pursuit halted, there was time for that.

At first sight the dart looked far from dangerous, being nothing more than a splinter of wood about the size of a matchstick with a sliver of glass fixed to one end. At the worst it could only have penetrated flesh by about half an inch. But there was more to the tiny projectile than that. Smeared on the glass tip was a sticky, dark-brown substance.

"Curare," Lee said woodenly. "Or the equivalent.

So now we know." He tossed the dart away. I dropped to my stomach, wriggled towards a large chunk of rock and raised my head carefully. Silver flashed by my face and another dart pinged harmlessly on the wall behind.

"We'll be all right as long as we keep our heads down," Lee said.

Which was true enough. And there was any amount of cover on our ledge. A stalemate seemed to exist. We were pinned down, and the pursuers, seemingly wary of more avalanches, had come to a halt. But they had all the advantages. With the sun burning down on our backs, we would soon be suffering the discomfort of thirst and would have to make a run for it. The ledge to the left seemed to offer a possible escape. I peered between two rocks at the men below. The injured man had been helped to his feet, but his arm hung loosely at his side. I wondered absently how they coped with sickness and injury in this dimension. It would certainly be very rough and ready.

Two of the men had moved away from the group and were engaged in some new activity. One was kneeling, holding across his bent elbows one of the larger, thicker bamboo tubes that I had earlier assumed to be a king-size version of the dart-weapon. His companion had produced a small skin bag, from which he was taking a variety of small objects that glistened brightly, catching and reflecting the sunlight. It was clear the two were assembling some kind of apparatus.

"What do you make of it?" Lee asked at my side.

I tried to disguise the fear in my voice. "I think we'll soon find out." I wondered if we ought to make a dash for it now. Two darts in quick succession, the moment I lifted my head a fraction, removed any hope.

The end of the wooden tube pointed in our direction like the muzzle of a gun. The stooping man fixed what was certainly a circular glass disc over the end of the threatening muzzle and then turned his attention to the other end of the tube, his back hiding what his hands were doing. As I watched with growing apprehension, the glass circle suddenly sprang into radiance as if a light had been switched on inside the tube. It increased in brilliance, becoming a flaring blue-white. And then the light seemed to elongate, projecting from the muzzle, moving slowly—a dazzling beam of light with a coiling rose-pink core. It came towards us, curving for all the world like an unbroken stream of tracer bullets, impinging on the rock a short distance below where we lay. And where it struck, rock glowed redly, hissing and bubbling like molten lava.

Reason lost in the face of this new, terrifying threat, I wriggled away from the verge of the ledge. Crouching to my feet, I turned, still bent double, to race as fast as I could along the ledge, only vaguely aware of a shape at my side that was Lee also running for his life.

A flash of light inches from my face was a dart, spending itself harmlessly against the rock. Others would be speeding towards us. But I had temporarily lost fear of them in the face of this new, terrifying weapon. All I knew was that I had to get as far away from that burning ray as possible.

From the side of my eye, as we ran along the ledge, I saw the beam sweeping across the rock face behind, leaving a trail of glowing, steaming lava in its wake. A clump of bushes burst into instant flame. Another dart sped by my face; something plucked at the sleeve of my shirt. The ledge had started to rise, slowing our stumbling progress. I slipped and almost fell. The bottom dropped out of my stomach as my feet slid beneath me. Recovering, I saw Lee a few paces ahead.

He hesitated, then vanished out of sight in a flurry of loose stones. For a moment I thought he had fallen from the ledge. But then in my turn I reached the end of the ledge to find a sudden dip that swung at the base to disappear into a narrow ravine.

I slithered down on my back in a cascade of rubble (as Lee must have done) to join him where he was picking himself up at the bottom. He helped me to my feet. Then we were racing along the ravine, skidding together round a corner. Reaching the end, we plunged into an unexpected but very welcome thicket of palms, thrusting the heavy leaves aside as we weaved our way between the thick grey trunks.

Emerging at the other side, we came to a gasping halt and turned to look back. We could see over the tops of the trees to the break in the hill-line that marked the ravine. There was no sign yet of pursuit. I wondered, drenched in sweat, my chest heaving painfully, reason returning, if they would have to dismantle their ray-weapon before following.

Still breathless, I was ready to move again. But not Lee. His hand was clamped to his side again.

"No," he shook his head. "It'll pass. Hell, it's like a knife jabbing." He was able to walk, but only slowly. There was nothing I could do to help apart from putting my arm about his waist, and that he objected to, shaking me away. But his teeth showed in a grin. "If I'd known what waited for me in this blasted place I'd have gone into training. I'll do better on my own, Gerald." He looked back over his shoulder. "Bloodhounds not in sight yet. That dry waterfall was a lucky break." He turned off his smile. "What price that damned heat-ray?"

We were making our way slowly over a level tract of ground. "I didn't think much about it," I said.

"Stone huts and fur jackets . . ." He paused for a moment and then stumbled on. "Glass plumbing and poison darts. And now a ray that by the way it churned up rock should be capable of burning through the thickest armour plating we have way back on earth. A hollow tree trunk, a few pieces of glass, and it turns out something like that. It just doesn't make sense. What kind of people are they?"

"God knows," I said.

"A damn crazy mixture of primitive and sophisticate." Taking his hand from his side, Lee said, "That's better," and looked back. I did too. A figure had topped the crest, silhouetted in the gap. Others followed.

Able to move quickly again, we finished crossing the open space and came upon more trees. One of the small furry animals squeaked alarm across our path, running with its belly close to the ground.

Out of the trees again and another open space to be crossed. But this one was encircled with a wall of rock, a wall that at the first, heart-sinking glance seemed unbroken, with no way over it or round it. But Lee, back in the lead again, found and made towards the narrow opening that had been hidden by a grotesque projection. Close on his heels I followed him into the welcome shade of towering walls. The floor was even, the going easy. Yet despite the pace we were keeping, the pursuit seemed to move even faster. We could hear voices shouting behind us.

The narrow passage opened up with dramatic suddenness to reveal an enclosed nightmare valley of desolate broken rock. On either side needles and pinnacles towered into the sky. Facing us, completely blocking the way, reaching from side to side, stretching up into the reddish haze of the sky, was a curtain of green-tinged mist.

We drew up sharply, aghast at the sight. I looked back. Nothing there except for the cleft we had just emerged from. It was the only way into the trap, the only way out. And voices echoed from it. Instinctive-ly we moved away from the sound, towards the mo-tionless mist.

"Between the devil and the deep blue sea," Lee said. "Do we risk that again"—he looked at the cur-tain—"or do we wait for our friends back there?"

To come and capture us again . . . But would it be their intention to make prisoners of us this time? Or, after the injury we had inflicted upon one of their number, would they come bursting out with weapons ready to fire? Would they use that infernal heat-ray against us again?

We stood there, backs to the mist, facing the threat of the cleft.

The first of our pursuers appeared in the opening, bamboo tube held across his chest. I can remember the way the sunlight flashed from the knife at his waist as he slid to a stop in a small flurry of dust. Two more men appeared, one of them carrying the larger tube of the heat-ray. And they too came to an abrupt halt.

They were not looking directly at us but over our shoulders towards the mist. And there was some-thing akin to fear on their squat swarthy faces. For a long moment we stood there, looking at them, wait-ing for their next move. Lee had gripped my elbow and I could feel the way his fingers bit into my flesh.

It was the figure with the dart-weapon who made the first move. He tore his eyes away from the mist, blinked at us, and then started to bring up his weap-on. That move made me aware of, and broke the spell of, the feeling of lassitude that had been creeping over me.

We turned together, Lee's grip still tight on my arm, and fled from the threat of poison darts and heat-ray towards the unknown and whatever might be waiting behind the the mist.

CHAPTER EIGHT

In the instant before reaching the curtain of mist I threw one last quick glance back over my shoulder. Lee was right behind me, almost blotting out the scene. But I caught a glimpse of the group of men at the opening of the ravine, more of them now—perhaps a dozen or so—all standing there, making no attempt to follow.

Then I turned my head back again and was in the mist. It is difficult to recall what happened then. I can remember being surprised that there was a sensation of solidness, that instead of feeling cold dampness on my face, instead of being able to plunge through it without obstruction, I felt a warm tingling on my exposed flesh and a resistance that almost brought me to a halt. It was the invisible resistance found in a nightmare race away from horror when one's panic-stricken pace is reduced to slow motion.

There was a smell, the same warm, sickly animal smell I had noticed before and had come to associate with the mist. Blinded by the enveloping greeny-greyness I had the impression of being held, of being picked up bodily and suspended in mid-air while walls closed in on either side. The substance that enclosed and held me became thicker and darker, blotting out what little light remained. The tingling on face and hands became more acute. I closed smarting eyes. There was the feeling of something draining the life out of my body, but that was a sensation that could only have lasted for a moment. Then the walls seemed to move back, the barrier in front ceased resisting and I dropped, or seemed to drop, lurching forward, stumbling, falling to my knees. The prickling stopped and I opened my eyes to find myself peering through floating tendrils of mist at a nightmare landscape of dim but hideous pools of seething matter, gigantic bubbles rising to the surface, bursting, sending up trails of vapour that drifted about the ghost-shapes of grotesque pinnacles of rock and tortured, leafless trees. The revolting stench caught at the back of my throat and burned in my nostrils. The terrifying, alien horror of the scene was indescribable. There was the feeling of being on another planet an infinity of space and time away from my own world, even from Dimension A. I felt the very ground under my knees writhe, as if it were alive, as if I were kneeling on the skin-shuddering back of some enormous creature. Fighting rising sickness, I closed my eyes against the horror and put my hands in front of my face—as if the action would afford some kind of protection. I couldn't have been far from unconsciousness.

Gradually the nausea passed. Behind my closed eyes I was aware of a change. The evil smell had gone and there was warmth on my shoulders. Taking

my hands from my face I opened my eyes. The nightmare scene had gone. I was kneeling on the emerald
grass of a glade with the familiar artificial trees and
bushes and flowers all about me. And in the distance
the bird was trilling its soft eerie notes.

Just behind me Lee was sitting up and gazing about
in stupefaction. Beneath the coating of sweat-caked
dust his features were strained. His eyes, meeting
mine, were glazed.

"Are you all right?" I asked anxiously.

He nodded, trying to square his shoulders. He tried
to speak, failed, tried again. "That was nasty while it
lasted. I think I must have passed out. I can't remember much about it, only that stuff, whatever it is, taking hold of me. It wasn't like ordinary mist . . ."

I waited for him to say something about that first
hideous scene. But he didn't, and when I asked him
he shook his head, saying he had seen nothing like
that. "And I don't think I was that far gone. You're
sure you saw it?" He looked round. "Here—where
all this is?"

The trees and bushes were all around us; even the
mist had vanished.

"Where all this is," I said.

He came to his feet. "Like I said, I almost passed
out."

"I was conscious. It wasn't a dream."

"Another puzzle then. I wouldn't like to have to go
through that experience again. A bit like coming
through the door. Remember? The same sort of feeling of being turned inside out."

I pushed myself upright. "Not much to choose between them for unpleasantness," I agreed.

"And we know one's artificial. A magnetic field.
So—"

"Not ordinary mist," I said. "Not even mist produced artifically. Some kind of force field perhaps.

And whatever it is, I don't think the people out there have had anything to do with it. They looked scared as far as I could tell. They had us cornered, there for the taking, but they just stood as if frightened to come any further."

"Conclusion:"—he mused—"two different forms of life. Those fellows out there and something that lives in here behind the mist or the force field, whichever it is. Something or some people who are able to produce solid hallucinations. Like all this now. Which could mean that if you weren't dreaming, what you saw was their real home before they got to work dolling it up for our benefit."

"I didn't dream it. You could be right, Lee. And if you are, and they bear any resemblance to their native surroundings, then I wouldn't much care to meet one of them face to face."

"They've done us no harm so far," he said. "The reverse if anything. It seems they've gone to the trouble to change their scenery into something they know we'll find more congenial. They're trying in their own way to make us feel at home. Last time we were in here they laid water on for us. Even if we didn't take advantage of it. Maybe, if that storm hadn't blown up, they'd have laid on food as well. They're offering hospitality. But why the hell do they keep out of sight?"

He scratched the stubble on his chin.

"Invisible? Is that it? They're here all the time, all around us. I can feel them watching us."

And so could I. There was that same neck-tingling sensation of being studied or carefully examined, as if the dark places under the trees harboured rows of inquisitive, intent eyes.

This could have been the same glade we had found ourselves in that other time. If it wasn't the same, then it was identical, even to the path that led through the trees, the only way out of the emerald circle.

"Another safari?" asked Lee.

I didn't reply. In my mind I was going back over ground we had already covered, wondering if there was some way we could prove at least part of our theory. We were being watched—that was for sure. By people—or things—able to look inside our minds, read the thoughts there, and then turn those mental images into a fair semblance of reality. In my mind they had found a picture of my home. But only of the outside. If I had been thinking about the inside, my bedroom, Mother's proud front room that she always called the "parlour," then the home they had made for my benefit wouldn't have been just an empty shell. I debated the possibility of trying an experiment by deliberately forming a picture of something in my mind. But then it occurred to me that, able to read my present thoughts, they would know what my intentions were and would perhaps refuse to allow themselves to be the subject of such an experiment. They might even take exception to it,

And what sort of beings were they? Unusual mental powers. And with the technical ability to enclose themselves in some kind of force field. I was sure that was what the mists were.

But why that shield at all? What were they protecting themselves against? Certainly not the fur-clad denizens of the rest of this dimension, for they had been frightened at even the sight of the mist.

My train of reasoning moved another step up the ladder. The fact that we had been allowed to penetrate their defense surely proved they knew we could do them no harm. More: the first time we had found ourselves in the artificial woods they had created, we had not entered of our own accord. They had sent us to sleep and, while we slept—I felt sure this was what had happened—they had moved their shield forward, parting it when it reached us, closing it behind us once we were inside. Don't come to visit my house, let me bring my house to you . . . And why had they done that? Curiosity, perhaps. Then the storm had come, and for some reason they had withdrawn the force field to leave us outside again. And then made another attempt to enclose us, one we had foiled by running away. Now we were back inside again. They had allowed us through—sanctuary from the danger outside. I could find no reason in the sequence of comings and goings.

I wondered if the path was the only way out of the glade, or if it was possible to force a way through the bushes and trees. It was, I felt, worth the effort of finding out if our movements in here were being deliberately controlled. After three attempts to find a way through the undergrowth (watched with raised eyebrows by Lee) I gave up. It was patently clear that if we wanted to leave the glade, the only way was by using the path. Lee was waiting for me at the entrance.

"And what was all that in aid of, Gerald?"

I told him as we walked.

"A guided tour," said he. "We go in the direction they want us to go or not at all. That's been obvious from the first."

It was a pleasant path to follow. The cool, green and gold shade was soothing. The soft green turf was resilient beneath our feet. Under any other conditions than these it would have been an enjoyable stroll. And oddly enough, although I knew we were at the mercy of something unknown, a feeling of placid contentment started to build up inside me. There was reassurance in the soundless padding of our feet, in the semi-hypnotic movements of tree trunks sliding by, vistas melting and changing like the shifting patterns of a kaleidoscope. I yawned. Aware that we had slowed our pace I still found nothing to worry about. Everywhere was silent, no breeze to ruffle the leaves, no bird-song. We were the only moving things. I was utterly at peace with myself and the world.

Lee's voice startled me.

"Four dials," he said slowly, tonelessly. "The top one indicates overloading. Two of the others have fixed readings, adjusted before the sequence starts. The third dial represents the current intake—"

He broke off, staring round him dazedly. I realised we were standing still.

Lee put one hand to his forehead. "Was that me?"

"You must have been daydreaming. You were back in the lab by the sound of it."

"I can't remember." He shook his head as if trying to clear his thoughts. "I don't think I was daydreaming. I must have been, though. My own voice woke me. Asleep on my feet."

We set off again. The path meandered along. Each corner we turned revealed a similar scene ahead. I had the uncanny feeling that we were marking time, that it was the scenery that was on the move, not we, the trees sliding by while we remained in the same place.

And it was getting dark, I suddenly realised. The sunlight that filtered through the branches overhead was losing its brightness. Shadows were deepening. The lassitude was back so that it became an effort to put one foot in front of the other. With it was the dream-like sensation of being suspended above the surface of the ground, walking on nothing, but that nothing clinging to my feet, retarding them, slowing my pace. Lee was a vague shape at my side, his voice coming from far away, the words too faint to be distinguishable. In a small surge of alarm I shouted to him. I opened my mouth, formed words, but no sound came.

Then the darkness became complete. I hung alone in emptiness. Something was deep inside my mind, twisting and writhing. I lurched forward through some vast, echoing place—echoing although there was no sound. My outstretched hands grasped desperately at nothing. I was falling, falling . . . And then blinding light came, and I could see again.

This was a dream. There could be no other explanation. I had fallen asleep, was dreaming, and was aware that I was dreaming. The woodland path had gone. Underfoot was the uneven hardness of cobbled stones. I had paused to wind my watch and now I was continuing across the farmyard to the squat grey building that housed the laboratory.

With no memory of opening the door, of passing through the outer room, I was in the lab itself, with Lee, shirt sleeves rolled up, turning to grin at me before entering his latest readings.

I was standing by the generators, the heat rising in waves . . . I was walking across the room, dislodging the wooden indicator with a careless foot. Knowing what was going to happen, but with no way of avoiding it, I was stooping to replace it, and the filaments were glowing inches from my face.

I shouted, as I had that other time, when I felt the grip of power. Lee's stool was flying and he was coming towards me. I felt his hand gripping my ankle and then I was plunging through the dancing screen of light, dragging him with me.

CHAPTER NINE

It was the same as it had been that first time, only now I knew what was happening, what was going to happen. Preparedness brought no relief to the sickening nightmare sensation of plunging down through darkness into some bottomless abyss. There was the same terrifying feeling of some power reaching inside me, lifting me out of myself, twisting me, replacing me. I wasn't prepared, for all I knew it was coming, for the body-jarring shock of striking ground. I was unable to prevent myself from lurching forward, falling, and rolling over and over until brought to a halt by some invisible obstruction.

The grey streaks of dawn were already in the brightening sky, which changed more rapidly than the first time, as if speeded up for my benefit. I had to go through the motions of turning to look back up the hill in search of the door, knowing all the time that it wouldn't be there.

And with that repetition came an end to the duplication of past events. Something seemed to withdraw from my mind, leaving my actions my own again. It was broad daylight now. I sat up and looked about me. A few yards away Lee was crouching on his knees. Between us was our cairn of stones, and all around was the familiar barren landscape of raw red rock, leafless shrubs, and stunted trees. And there as well, hanging at the far side of the open space, was the green-tinged curtain of mist.

On his feet, swaying a little, Lee gestured helplessly. "Back where we came in . . ." And then angrily, savagely: "I'm damn well fed up with being messed about. The hell with it!" He glared about him.

Coming to my feet I kept a wary eye on the curtain. It seemed to be moving towards us again. Rock formations—one of them my pyramid and spire arrangement—that had been visible when the light first came were no longer there. There was no need for me to cry a warning. Lee had spotted it for himself.

"No you damn well don't!" he hurled at the mist. And then, sliding and skidding on a patch of loose rock, he moved in the opposite direction to that we had taken the first time we had fled from the creeping curtain. It took me a moment to catch up with him. His fury had worn off; his grin was only partly shamefaced.

"I feel all the better, anyway." He looked back. The mist was still visible, but at a safe enough distance. "I wonder if they heard me?"

He made no comment about our latest experience, and I didn't bring the subject up. Talking about it would get us nowhere. Not now, not while we needed all our breath for the rough road we were travelling.

It was the familiar desolate wilderness of raw red rock and stunted trees and scrub that seemed to form the greater part of the scenery of this world. Dust rose in a fine red cloud about our feet, and drifting, settled on the sticky sweat of faces and hands. The sun beat down with tropical intensity.

We had left the hill where we had first arrived. Passing between two huge boulders we found ourselves on the brink of a large, crater-like depression. Standing at one side was a clumsy-looking construction of lengths of tree trunk lashed together, a crude scaffolding with a platform on top that was about eight feet square. The contraption stood about six feet from the ground, and rough ladders made of shorter lengths of wood were attached to each side.

"Used when they're building houses?" Lee rested his arms on a flat piece of rock. "No—not that shape. Could be some kind of look-out post, but it isn't, not stuck down there in a hollow. Shall we?"

We skated down loose scree and walked across to the primitive construction. It reminded me of something, incongruous though the notion was.

"Wembley," I said. "For leading the crowd in community singing on cup final day."

He grinned. "A far cry from Wembley Stadium. But I see the resemblance. Shall we try six verses of 'Land of Hope and Glory'?" He set his foot on one of the ladders and the contraption rocked alarmingly.

He stepped back.

"Whoever threw it together didn't make a very good job of it. You've only got to touch it—" Then he discovered why it was so unstable. "Two of the legs are at least a foot shorter than the others." He rubbed his jaw. "Why, for Pete's sake?"

"They're fond of building things on a slope," I said. "Like the walls of their houses."

"We're only assuming our fur-clad friends built this. I suppose they did . . . And after seeing their heat-ray in action I've changed my mind about their capabilities. If they're clever enough to invent a weapon like that, then I'm damned sure they're not stupid enough to build houses with sloping walls or a one-sided affair like this without good reason."

We climbed back out of the hollow and continued on our way to no place in particular, our prime concern for the time being to get away from the mist. Several dozen paces brought us to a bend in the path. In the lead, I rounded the corner warily. It was well I did. Another large hollow contained a score or more of the fur-clad men. Crouching, we peered down at them.

Four squatted on their haunches at the entrance to a cave. On the dusty ground at their side was a large neatly-stacked pile of the larger heat-ray tubes. Alongside was another pile, this one made up of the accompanying animal-skin bags which we knew from the past must contain the glass sections of the weapons—presumably lenses and mirrors.

The remainder of the men were dotted about the lower slopes of the surrounding hills—some walking slowly, others standing still, all armed with the dart-guns.

"Settlement of cave dwellers?"—Lee hazarded softly. "I shouldn't think so. No women for one thing. Hunting party? Not with that collection of heavy armament. Search party?"

And at first that seemed the reasonable answer. They had been sent out after us but decided to rest. They stacked the heavy stuff and then, perhaps with some of their number out scouting, were taking things easy for a while.

But whatever the reason for their presence here, there was no going through them or round them. We moved carefully back, turned, and retraced our steps along the rim of the first hollow, striking away at an angle when we came to a break in the rock.

And now the terrain seemed to be even more rugged. With no path, it was a case of following the line of least resistance, skirting the unscalable rocks, climbing the smaller. The food we had eaten earlier kept hunger more or less at bay, but thirst had long ago started to make itself felt. As the red haze in the sky slowly cleared, the sun blazed down more fiercely than ever. We stopped after a harder climb than usual and, hugging the meagre shade of a low escarpment, rested and looked about us. There seemed no break in the lunar landscape of red rock. In all directions it reached away to be lost in the shimmering heat haze.

It is impossible to say how long we struggled on before coming upon a change of scenery. I would guess that the best part of two hours had passed from the time of our leaving the twin hollows to the moment when, only able to move slowly now, we emerged from a narrow ravine to find a well-defined path in front of us. With relief we turned to follow it, hoping the path would lead to water. It climbed a smooth-topped hill, was lost on the summit, reappeared as a brown ribbon across the unhappy green of a stretch of grass, swung away, dipped into an unexpected hollow and vanished into a thicket of palms.

There was great relief in the shade of the entwined leaves overhead, even with the return to the inevitable back-bent progress. We paused to rest and, resting, heard in the silence the soft rustle of water. We easily traced it to its source. And this was a larger stream than the other we had made use of, wider, spanned by a crude wooden bridge.

This time, parched though we were, we approached with caution. And we took turns to drink and bathe our faces, Lee keeping watch while I made the most of the ice-cold water, I later doing the same for him. Then for a while we sat in the shade of a group of trees.

And we came round to talking about the hallucination—for that is what it must have been, an artificially induced hallucination—that had caused us to relive the transition from our world to this dimension. Thinking about it, brooding upon it in a desultory fashion as we struggled along under the sun, I had come up with a possible explanation. One that tied in with my private assessment of the nature of the invisible beings who lived behind the mist.

"Curiosity," I said. "That seems to be behind everything they do. When we first came they gathered us in to try to find out what sort of beings we were. And then they wanted to find out where we came from and how we got here."

"A hell of a way to go about picking one's brain," Lee said resentfully. "Making us live through that a second time. Why the blazes don't they just come out into the open and ask?"

"Perhaps they can't." I pulled up my trouser leg to inspect a bruised knee. "We think of living things in terms of our own world. People, animals, plants. It could be the things that live inside the mist are a different form of life altogether, something beyond even our imagination."

"I had an idea they might be invisible," he said as I pulled the trouser leg down again. "I'm sure they can't be, though. Look at it this way. They can read thoughts. That means they have brains. Brains have to have containers. That means they have bodies. It stands to reason."

Reason . . . What use was reason here? It could only be applied to abstract things—motives. And even then it was wild guesswork. The only thing I could be sure about was that they were curious about

us. And that, after all, was common sense, not reason.

Pushing myself upright I looked at the sky, shielding my eyes against the sun's glare. The molten blinding disc was well to one side now. If there was any
parallel between time here and that in our world,
then I guessed it must be about four o'clock. I of-
ferred the estimate to Lee for something new to
say, something to change a topic that could lead to
useless discussion and even argument. I had read
somewhere that heat can make people touchy and
short-tempered. I could well believe it now.

"Four o'clock," he echoed dismally. "Tea-time.
Maybe where we're standing now there's a lawn all
set out with tables and chairs and the Sunday-best
crockery, with the vicar doing his stuff and handing
round the muffins. God . . ."

"Time we were on the move again," I said.

He didn't ask where we intended moving to. Deep
in thought—perhaps brooding on the tea-party he
had dreamed up—he followed as I crossed the
bridge. I went even more cautiously now, assuming
that a well-used path and a bridge indicated a settlement nearby.

And a settlement meant food. In my mind I was
formulating a plan of sorts. Ever since we had been
in this place we had been badgered from pillar to
post without a chance to set about doing anything
constructive. We seemed to have spent the greater
part of our time on the run. It was high time we got
ourselves organised. I shelved the telling of my plan
for the time being because it would certainly give
rise to discussion. And right now it was best we keep
as quiet as possible.

I was right in my assumption that we were close
to a village. We weaved our way between more
palms, negotiated a narrow ravine, and came out on

a narrow ledge. The ledge overlooked a saucer-shaped hollow containing a settlement that was almost a duplicate of the one where we had been held prisoners. It was so alike that at first I thought it was our original village, that we had simply approached it from another direction. But as we edged down the slope—any amount of cover in the shape of trees and rock outcroppings—it became obvious that this was a different, much larger settlement.

"A veritable city," Lee said in the pause, before moving to the next cover.

We had seen from the ledge only a few of the outlying houses. In all, there must have been well over a hundred, all identical in appearance. The stream snaked between them to end at a small central lake. There was little sign of the occupants of the houses. Figures moved about, but there were no groups. A few children played at the water's edge. A solitary woman, crouched in the shadow of one of the houses, pounded with stone pestle in stone mortar. Smoke trailed unwaveringly into the sky from a fire that was out of sight.

Lee and I changed position, moving to where a patch of grass provided a reasonably comfortable resting place and where two palms and a pile of rock gave both shade and cover. Lying flat on our stomachs we contemplated the village.

It was time to unfold my plan. If we kept our voices down we would be safe enough. Rolling over so that I could keep an eye on our rear, I started by pointing out that we had achieved very little since our arrival in this dimension.

"I wouldn't exactly say that," Lee grunted. "We've learned quite a lot, one way and another."

"But what we've learned is no use to us, not the way we are. The whole idea of finding the way into this dimension was so that we could rescue your uncle and his assistant."

"You don't have to remind me of that."

"But we came through unprepared."

"Nor that." He squinted sideways at me. "What's this leading to?"

I told him, speaking quickly, allowing no space for interruption.

"We can't do anything like this. We've got to go back and start all over again. First we get food and water. The village here should be able to provide both, and something to carry the water in. Then we make our way back to the hill and wait for the door to open. We find somewhere to hide, out of the sun, away from the mist and out of sight of the men there. When the door opens, as it's bound to sooner or later, we go through. And then we come back again, only this time properly organised and equipped, maybe with help—Mr. Leming, perhaps. With suitable clothing, supplies, even guns if we can get hold of them. Then we'll stand a good chance of finding Professor Maver."

I had expected objections, strong ones, that would lead to argument. It wasn't like that at all. Leo seized upon one of my suggestions.

"Guns. Yes. Shotguns. I know a farmer who'd lend us a couple of those and cartridges, without asking questions. That would shake those boys with their heat-rays."

He was clearly much enamoured of the notion. He spent a few moments in reflection, almost certainly visualising shotguns in action against heat-rays and poison darts.

Then: "Yes, Gerald. Like you say, we're helpless the way we are. Common sense instead of heroics is the thing. All right. Something to carry water . . . I don't fancy mountain climbing hampered with glass ewers."

"Water isn't piped into the houses. They must have some way of bringing it from the streams. They're bound to have something apart from the jugs."

"A touch of Sherlock Holmes." He grinned. "Fair enough. So, suitably fitted out, we find our way back to the hill. And with a bit of luck the door appears. Suspended—what?—four or five feet in mid-air? Do we fly through?"

"It didn't take long to build the cairn. We've got a fairly good idea where the door must be. So we build another cairn, only much larger."

"And hope it's in the right place."

In the circular valley two more trails of smoke had come to join the first. Evening meals being prepared, I thought. A party of fur-clad men were making their way towards the houses, coming down the slopes at the far side of the settlement. There were perhaps a score of them and they all had leathery-looking bags, heavy by the way they were being carried.

"Getting food and something to carry water in will be the trickiest part," I said. "We'll have to wait for darkness."

"When they're all tucked up in bed." Lee looked up at the sky. "And when is that likely to be? How long are the days in this place?"

"By the rate the sun is moving I'm guessing they're about the same duration as ours."

The laden men had reached the village and were dispersing. Some women had appeared, going to join the children who played at the lake side. Two men walked together on the outskirts of a cluster of houses, one much taller than the other—a head taller, and with something peculiar about his clothing. I shielded my eyes against the slanting sun. The two had stopped at the door of one of the houses, the taller turning in our direction as he reached to open the door. Then I saw what was strange about his clothing. He was wearing an ordinary jacket and trousers.

And Lee exclaimed excitedly, "Uncle John!" On his knees, then on his feet, Lee would, I think, have gone pelting down the slope there and then if I hadn't managed just in time to tackle him round the waist and drag him back down behind the rocks.

He struggled. Then relaxed. I took my hands away.

"It won't do any good dashing down there like that," I said. "He doesn't look as if he is being kept prisoner, but we can't tell for sure. And if they capture us again, we won't be able to help him."

He took a deep breath. "I didn't give myself time to think. Maybe I would when it was too late. I saw him there, and that was that . . . Sorry, Gerald."

He wriggled back to his viewing position, and I joined him. There was no sign of the Professor; I assumed he had gone into the house. His former companion was making his way back to the centre of the village. One thing was in our favour if we intended a rescue operation. The Professor's prison, if that was what it was, stood alone on the fringe of the place. And there was no guard on duty outside. I leaned forward to inspect the general lay of the land. It seemed to me that there was sufficient cover for us to make our way along the slopes that enclosed the valley and safely reach a point immediately behind a thicket of palms. We could snake our way down to those and then make a quick dash to the isolated house. Two hazards: we might be spotted during the manoeuvre, and the Professor might not be alone.

Lee had guessed what I had in mind. "What do

you think?" he asked anxiously. "Now—or when it's dark?"

"I think we can risk it now."

He must have been following the directions of my eyes. "Along the slope, down to the trees, then to the house?"

"That's it." I offered the snags.

"We should be hidden from the rest of the houses," he said. "And I think he'll be on his own. He didn't look like a prisoner to me. I mean, that bloke with him wasn't armed. They looked like two friends out for an evening stroll before turning in for the night."

We made our way along the slope, slipping from cover to cover. The going was easier than I had envisaged. We waited a few moments before making the little dash down to the palms. We waited again before the final race to the shadow at the rear of the house.

Lee, his back against the wall in approved fashion, inched along to the corner, peered round, nodded to me to follow and then moved on. The area in front of the house was deserted. There was no one to see our final dash to the door. Lee opened it and I followed him quickly inside.

The room was a duplicate of the one we had earlier escaped from. The man who sat on the chair looked up at our entrance, startled, mouth gaping. There was an odd little hiatus. Then he came to his feet.

"Dr. Livingstone, I presume," Lee said with a deplorable lack of originality, going to meet him.

CHAPTER TEN

My first impression of Professor Maver turned out to be a false one. But there was excuse enough for my wrong assessment. By his appearance, by his clothes in particular, I judged him to be a man of careless and untidy habits who gave little or no thought to his person. The typical absent-minded professor of fiction.

The threadbare tweed jacket that hung loosely from his lanky shoulders would have been more fitting on the wooden frame of a scarecrow. All the buttons were missing. The jacket was tied about the waist with cord. There were long, lining-exposing rents, one pocket flapped from its moorings, and one lapel had become almost completely detached. His flannels were in no better shape; a boney knee poked through the gaping hole in one leg. As far as I could see he wore nothing beneath the jacket. Certainly, his feet were bare.

His clothes, I felt sure, could never have gotten into such a state in the short time he had been in this place, even if he had suffered the roughest of rough passages out there in the hills. And neither could his thick, greying hair have grown to such a length, curling on his shoulders, in six short weeks. So here, I told myself, was a man slovenly about appearance. And how wrong I was. I was later to find that he was the very reverse of all this and that under normal circumstances he was always most fastidious about his appearance.

Tallness made him stoop a little, as it does many large men. His face was brick-red, and ugly—but pleasantly ugly—with over-large eyes and nose, with deep corrugations to the flesh of forehead and cheeks. He was possessed of a quiet humour, but that was something that wasn't in evidence at the first moment of the encounter. The shock of surprise had driven everything else away.

He shook hands with Lee, his other huge paw clamped on Lee's shoulder. Speechless, he pumped and beamed and nodded his head. It had been a very long six weeks for him.

"Well—" he exploded, and was lost for further words. "Well," he said again. Letting Lee's hand drop at last, he unclamped his grip and nodded afresh. And then seemed to see me for the first time, nodded yet again, smiled, and then furrowed a massive forehead in perplexity. The initial impact of the meeting was over. Lee introduced me, explaining briefly who I was.

And then the Professor launched a spate of questions.

Who had operated the field? he wanted to know. Was it still in operation? How long had we been here? Had anyone else come with us?

Lee did his best to cope.

"We came through this morning," he started "Just the two of us—just before daybreak. At least, daybreak here."

This was going to go on for a long time. I broke in: "Are we likely to be interrupted, sir?"

He stared at me impatiently. "Interrupted?"

"By the fur-clad boys," Lee enlarged. "We've had a spot of trouble with them once already. We don't want any more."

Maver was puzzled. "Trouble with the Toparians?"

"Never heard of them," Lee rejoined inelegantly.

"The people who live here. Toparians. But they're friendly. What has been happening?"

Lee treated him to a very shortened version of our encounter with the heat-ray.

"And they fired on you?" Maver was perplexed. "I can well understand them trying to round you up. That would be for your own good. But to use the ray on you . . . You must have angered them in some way." He broke off. "All that can wait. Tell me how you managed to operate the field."

"We got someone to do the trick for us," Lee told him. "Or rather, to start us on the way. I dragged in Gerald's boss—Mr. Leming."

"Martin Leming!" Maver was delighted. "You couldn't have chosen a better man. But you say only the two of you came through?"

"And by accident," Lee said wryly. "We fell rather than came. You see, after you and Adam disappeared—" He paused. "Where is Adam? Is he all right?"

The other nodded testily. "I should imagine so." And then: "But of course you don't know. These are Adam's own kind."

We both gaped at him.

Lee recovered first. "His own kind?"

"He's a Toparian," the Professor said. "I knew that

much about him before we started our experiments. He came through to our world, purely as the result of natural circumstances, about four and a half years ago."

"I can't believe it," Lee said. "And yet, his appearance . . . He's not all that much unlike the people here."

"I would have told you," Maver said, "but he asked me not to tell anyone. If the news had got out, and been believed—" He shrugged expressively. "It was mainly as a result of what he was able to tell me about the trio of happenings that was responsible for his coming to our world that I was able to duplicate the sequence in the laboratory. A sequence that obviously Leming was able to make sense of. You still haven't answered my first question, Lee. Is the field still in operation?"

"No. At least it wasn't two or three hours back. Gerald and I are guessing that it closed almost immediately after we had fallen through. And we're guessing that right now Mr. Leming will be doing his damnedest to get it open again. We've marked the place with a pile of stones."

Maver shook his head sadly. "It may take him a long time. It took me two years. But part of that time was spent in working out the two fixed frequencies."

"That's what Mr. Leming thought. It only took him a few hours to get the hang of it. But of course he had everything ready there in front of him. It took us—" He looked at me.

"We started working on the sequences on Wednesday," I said. "We hit the right combination on Saturday morning. This morning."

"Three days?" Maver's perplexity slid from my face to Lee's. "You only started three days ago? Why did you wait so long?"

Lee explained about the Special Branch intervention.

"I went along with his instructions for five weeks," he finished. "Then I felt it was time something was done. That's when I contacted Mr. Leming through Gerald."

There was something much more than perplexity on the Professor's face now. Something that verged on shock. But it was there for only a moment. Watching his face, noting the change of expression, I fancied I could almost see his mind at work behind his eyes.

"Have I been away for only five weeks?" he asked steadily. "Is that what you're trying to say?"

"It must have seemed much longer than that to you," Lee said sympathetically.

"It not only seemed much longer . . ."—there was a hint of dryness in Maver's voice—". . . it was. Much, much longer. They have no means of recording the passage of time in this place, no watches or clocks. And, because of the strong magnetic fields here, my watch is useless. You've probably found yours are useless too. But I have evolved a means of keeping note of the passing days, purely for my own convenience. The days here are almost the same length as those back on earth. An estimate only, of course, but a reasonably accurate one. Each day when the midday meal is brought, I use a spoon to scratch a mark on the sandstone wall." He nodded to the far wall. "You can see for yourself. And without having to go over to consult it I can tell you exactly how long I have been here. One year, one month and fourteen days."

This time it was Lee's and my turn to be stunned into silence.

"But that's impossible!" Lee burst out finally.

"I was expecting your disbelief," his uncle said

placidly. "I can vouch for the accuracy of my calculation. Some months ago I was ill for a few days. Sunstroke, I fancy. But I was able to carry on with my calendar. Let me see—" He closed his eyes for a moment of concentration. "Yes. A time ratio of roughly one to twenty. Which explains something that Adam found very puzzling. Why upon his return to his native village he was unable to find any familiar faces, why no one was able to recognise him. His four years plus in our world represented the passage of almost a century here. Two generations."

"A different time altogether." Lee nodded. "I can believe it now. After the things that have been happening to Gerald and me I can believe almost anything. What sort of place is this, Uncle John? We haven't been able to make much sense of it. There are the people here, the back-to-nature types, those you call Toparians. And then there are the weird things that go on inside the mist. What's it all about, for Pete's sake?"

"Inside the mist?" The Professor obviously knew what Lee was talking about, and yet was startled again. "What do you know about it?"

"Not much. For a start, we figured it must be some kind of artificial force field."

"You're not saying you've been behind it?"

"For our sins, twice." Lee grimaced. "Visitations we're not all that anxious to repeat. Not that whoever lives there did us any harm."

Maver said, "You're the first ones to go through the mist and come out alive. Unless my informant was lying, and I don't think she was."

He became aware that we were standing. "What am I thinking of?" The bench was long enough to accommodate Lee and me in comfort. Maver swung the chair round to face us and seated himself.

"I feel we can spare the time to bring each other

up to date. So far as you and your friend are concerned, Lee, I feel it is essential. Now that we are aware of the difference in the passage of time it looks as if you may be here for a while. Martin—Mr. Leming—will undoubtedly be doing his best to activate the field again. But one hour of his time is almost a day of ours.

"We won't be disturbed"—that was for my benefit; he nodded and smiled at me—"until they bring fresh water and the evening meal. That will be in about two hours' time. I am very anxious to hear what you found in the . . ."—he paused—"behind the mist. But it is far more important that you learn something about this place and the dangers it holds. And there are dangers, but not from the Toparians. They are a placid, friendly people.

"Adam and I came here by intent." Maver paused. "Perhaps that is incorrect. Let us say we intended to pass through the field, but our method of passage was accidental. It was certainly not a properly planned scientific expedition. You are obviously aware of the technique employed in activating the complex field. A system of trial and error, a duplicating of natural events. If 'natural' is the correct word. I had three things to duplicate. Two were straightforward enough. The third presented some difficulty. Adam, incidentally, was forced into our world by the accidental and natural combination of the three fields, but that is something I will enlarge upon later.

"It would be about nine in the morning when we found the final current sequence that completed the trio and activated the field. I won't dwell upon my feelings . . . Adam, naturally enough, was eager to go through immediately, without prior investigation. I managed to curb his enthusiasm, pointing out that we didn't know for certain that it was indeed his world that lay beyond the field. I persuaded him it was most essential we conduct some form of investigation. As it turned out, our efforts in this direction were of a most cursory nature.

"It soon became obvious that the field was far from stable. To maintain it at all meant continual adjustment of the apparatus. There was no way of telling how long we would be able to hold the field in position. This was something I had not envisaged, otherwise I could have made adequate preparations. As it was, we had to work quickly, improvising makeshift tools, adapted from anything that came to hand.

"I can recall being troubled when the wooden stave we used as the first probe failed to strike anything solid. It occurred to me then that there might be a variance between the ground level of the laboratory and that which lay beyond the field.

"As the day wore on with our investigations producing no result, Adam became increasingly impatient. It was his idea that he go through with the precaution of a safety rope tied about his waist. For a while I was reluctant to allow him to do that. But it was becoming progressively more difficult to keep the power steady. It seemed to me that some unknown factor must be involved. As it turned out, I was correct. A magnetic storm (fortunately only a small one, not unlike the one we experienced earlier today) was raging here.

"Late in the afternoon the field started to waver alarmingly. I am assuming this was caused by the after-effect of the storm. I was unable to restrain Adam any longer. With the rope tied about his waist he went through the field. Braced as I was for any sudden pressure, I was still caught off balance. I fell through, as you must have done, and rolled down the hill. It was a little while before I had recovered sufficiently to take an interest in my surroundings. I was vastly relieved when Adam confirmed that this was indeed his world. I was perturbed when, looking back, I saw that there was no sign of the field. And that happened over a year ago."

"Or six weeks," Lee supplied. "Depending where you happen to be. The adjustable section of your equipment was burnt out."

"I assumed something of that nature must have happened. The passage of our bodies through the field created the means for the aftermath magnetic surge of the storm to also pass through, so overloading my system. The same thing probably happened, but on a reduced scale, when you came through. That is something I must rectify in the future. It will simply mean an adjustment to the safety device."

I hoped, but didn't pass the comment, that he would find himself in a position of being able to make that adjustment.

Lee looked round the room. "And they've kept you here ever since?"

"Not 'kept,' Lee. I'm more or less free to come and go as I please."

"Only more or less?"

"This is far from being a hospitable world," Maver explained. "It is subject to violent magnetic storms which arise with very little warning. To be caught out in the open when a bad one breaks would be fatal. Sometimes we have two or three storm-free days on the run. Another day might mean as many as a score of storms during the daylight hours alone. One does not move far from the houses unless one is very familiar with the country and knows where shelter may be obtained. Another hazard is an unpleasant shrub that flourishes among the rocks—"

"Thorny-looking affairs," Lee said. "We've been giving them a wide berth."

"It is as well you have," the Professor said. "The plant is obviously a modified form of something that grew here before the Magnetic War. The spines are extremely dangerous. A scratch from one will induce paralysis and unconsciousness. The Toparians use a substance extracted from the roots to tip their darts."

"Which we have also met," Lee said dryly. "So the weather has kept you confined to barracks. And where has Adam been all this while?"

Maver leaned forward, frowning.

"I have no idea. I have viewed his prolonged absence with mixed feelings. After our long association in our world I would have expected to see quite a lot of him here. On the other hand, I told myself that he was perhaps wrapped up in his own affairs.

"During the time we were working together in my laboratory he was inclined to be reticent about his home, talking very little about it, and then only with reluctance. I remember his once saying that the civilization he came from was vastly inferior to ours. I felt that he was ashamed to talk about the conditions under which he had once had to exist. It was only natural that I was curious about his world. But I didn't press questions on him. I felt that he would tell me all about it in his own good time.

"What I had managed to learn about this place and its history I have picked up from the woman who brings the midday meal. A pleasant-enough female, if lacking in intelligence. From her I have managed to learn enough of the language to be able to understand most of what she tells me.

"At Haweford, when I first came to know Adam for what he really was, he told me that he was a person of some importance in his own country. Some kind of chieftain, I gathered. The word suggested a tribe, confirmed that his civilization was far behind ours.

"When we first arrived here, he led me to this village. He was astonished and dismayed to find all the faces strange. We know now why they were strange. He spoke to the people, telling them who he was and where he had been. A little later I was escorted to this house where I have been ever since. Adam told me that arrangements had been made for a watch to be kept on the hill. I would be informed if and when the field reappeared. The arrangement struck me as being sensible. Doubts started to come when the days passed with no further sign of Adam. I put them aside, telling myself that if he was indeed an important person here, then he would have much to occupy his time. But now those doubts are flooding back . . ."

"Surely it couldn't have taken him long to find out why all the faces were strange," Lee said. "He would talk to people, find familiar names. He'd soon find out about the difference in times."

The other nodded worriedly. "I realise that now. It is also significant that today no word has been sent me about the reappearance of the field or of your arrival. The former could have escaped notice. But certainly not the latter."

He lapsed into a brooding silence. Lee rose from the bench, hoisted himself to the table, and crossed his legs.

"All," he observed, "is not right in the state of Denmark. Something stinks. Or would seem to. Time is slipping by, Uncle John. Your lady-friend or who-ever brings supper will soon be here. And we're anxious to find out about the mist."

"Yes." Professor Maver roused himself. "The Korved Circles. And to know about those means going back to the start, to the Magnetic War."

CHAPTER ELEVEN

"They call this world 'Korva,' " said Professor Maver. "The equivalent of our word 'Earth.' It exists in a completely different universe from ours. The night sky is unrecognisable: there are two moons; the constellations are all strange. But there are certain similarities between this dimension and ours. Korva must be of exactly the same size as Earth, otherwise surface passage between the two would be impossible. The sun is much like ours, and so is Korva's rotation about it."

He paused after the preliminaries.

"I had assumed for a long time that some of the people who vanish from Earth find their way here. It is an assumption that has been proved correct. The doorway between the two dimensions is, as you are well aware, a field comprised of three magnetic forces. I produced the resultant complex field artificially in my laboratory. Under certain conditions they are produced here naturally.

"It is difficult to explain without using technicalities. The mists are, as you have correctly deduced, force fields. They can be called the equivalent of one of the poles on the laboratory floor. The strong magnetic field of this world constitutes the second. Add the final pole-equivalent, a magnetic storm, and you have the necessary conditions to breach the dividing wall. Am I making myself clear?"

"Abundantly so," Lee said.

"Good. When these three fields come in contact with each other, any person who happens to be standing on the precise spot in our world is drawn through. It is as simple as that. Unfortunately the human frame is not strong enough to withstand the experience. Those that are drawn through have been subjected to forces infinitely more powerful than those produced in the laboratory. They are always dead upon arrival here. Their bodies, of course, always appear close to the mists. Many are in some way absorbed by the mist. The Korvans recover the rest, and, by the clothing and personal effects, know that they have come from some place other than Korva. Long ago the Korvans came to the conclusion that there must be another world nearby. When Adam and I came through, there was no surprise at our appearance, only amazement that we were alive.

"The traffic between the two dimensions isn't entirely one-way. Adam made the journey in the opposite direction—a rare occurrence. He was alone, out hunting. There is a small animal here (perhaps another modification of life that existed before the destruction of the Magnetic War) which the Korvans hunt mainly for its skin."

"We've seen them," Lee inserted.

"There are few enough of them, and so they are

much in demand. Pursuing one of them, Adam came nearer to the mist than safety demands. He slipped and, catching his foot between two stones, badly bruised his ankle. Fortunately, he was still able to walk. The ankle-covering these people wear—a protection against the spines of the shrub—saved him from any real hurt. But before he was able to limp away, a storm broke. Unprotected, he became unconscious. When he came round again, the storm was still raging. Not until it had passed over did he realise he was no longer in his own world. He guessed what had happened. Most of his clothing had been ripped away by the magnetic storm. He knew, because of the bodies he had seen of people who had come the other way through the wall, that in appearance he would be like the denizens of this new world. But he wouldn't be able to speak their language. And he had no way of knowing if they would be friendly. He decided to be very cautious.

"Adam found himself in a field, not far from a farm. He staggered towards the buildings, but collapsed before reaching them. When he came round again, he found himself in hospital. He learned afterwards that the farmer who had found him had assumed he had been struck by lightning. And in the hospital, when he didn't speak and didn't seem to understand what was being said to him, the people assumed he had lost his memory.

"During the three months he was a patient he picked up a smattering of English, enough to enable him to obtain a job on a farm. Aware of his accent and somewhat foreign appearance, he assumed the name Adam Sokel, a name that could have originated anywhere in Europe. After a year and a half, when he was able to read English as well as speak it fluently, Adam read one of my articles on my development of Einstein's theory of simultaneous worlds. I suggested the possibility of being able to contact the nearest of these other worlds. Adam came to see me, asking for work. I took him on—first as gardener, then as handyman. And after a while, when he had come to discover that I was seriously considering attempting to contact Dimension A, he told me who he really was. His one desire was to return to his own world. I was the one man who might be able to help."

"And you did," Lee said bleakly. "And now that you're in the same boat, he goes and leaves you flat."

"So it would appear." Maver rubbed the heavy creases of his forehead with a huge finger. "But we mustn't condemn him out of hand. Something may have happened to him. We must wait . . .

"What little I have managed to learn about this world has been through the good offices of my lady visitor. It isn't her fault that her knowledge of the past is very sketchy. The Toparians obey something they call the New Law. It is a series of instructions that bars progress, prohibiting among other things the use of metal in any shape or form. Since the Toparians have no means of recording the past—not even writing materials—history has come down by word of mouth only. And so has suffered distortion, which means it is difficult to separate legend from fact.

"Korva is similar to Earth in that it is divided into land masses separated by seas. This country is called Topar. Oddly, this history of the Toparians bears some resemblance to that of the British. They had their Agricultural Revolution when they came to re- alise that the over-worked land would soon be un- able to produce sufficient crops to feed a rapidly ex- panding population. Their Industrial Revolution was an extension of the Agricultural, based on the need to manufacture machinery for producing artificial fertilizers. Then came a third revolution, comparable with our present Nuclear Age. One could call it the Magnetic Revolution.

"Earth has its magnetic fields. Korva has them too, and, even before the Magnetic War, infinitely stronger than Earth's. The Korvans learned how to put the fields to use. They used magnetism to drive their machines and power their aircraft and vehicles. And finally, inevitably, they constructed weapons.

"First one country, then another, finally all, built and tested magnetic weapons. And after a while the ordinary people, alarmed, voiced protest, banding themselves into groups for the purpose."

"Ban the Bomb," I said. "The Campaign for Nuclear Disarmament. Protest marches."

"A parallel with our world indeed," agreed the Professor. "And a harsh lesson for us to learn. Here, on Korva, the people organised themselves on a vast scale. The various groups combined to form the one Society. The Society created its own code of laws, the same code the people abide by now. A stern, unbending law, first promulgated in self-defence, that now bars the way to progress. Its original intention was to abolish not only the magnetic weapons, but also every piece of machinery, every plane and vehicle that used magnetism as its driving force. But the efforts of the Society proved unsuccessful. Perhaps they had waited too long before organising themselves. War broke out, and the magnetic weapons were used."

Maver paused.

"Here it becomes difficult to differentiate between legend and history. There seems no clear information as to the actual nature of the weapons. Certainly, they were not bombs as we know them. Legend speaks of the Time of the Great Roaring Whirlpools. This leads me to suspect that the weapons were devices that increased and distorted the natural magnetic fields. They would be dropped from the air with the centres of densest populations as the main targets. The havoc they caused—and there can be no doubt about this—was comparable to the wholesale destruction that would be caused by the dropping of a hydrogen bomb. Within a certain radius there was complete annihilation. The effects spread outwards, killing every living thing on the planet's surface, vapourising everything, so that not a building was left standing.

"Only a small number of people managed to survive. The survivors formed two distinct classes. There were those people who lived out in the wilds and who were able to find large and deep enough caves in which first to seek refuge and afterwards to live. And there were those city-dwellers who were able to survive in the artificial deep shelters.

"Unlike bombs, the magnetic devices did not have instantaneous effects. The process of annihilation continued over a very long time, probably for many years. One can visualise the enormous vortices of destruction, the huge tornadoes reaching high into the air, the roaring whirlpools of legend."

The Professor spread his hands.

"Civilisation was wiped out. The few survivors lived as best they could in their shelters. After a long time, when the devices had finally died, the cave-dwellers emerged. The Toparians are their descendants. Of the others, there is little reliable information. Here, legend has completely taken over. They are the people who live inside the mists. No one has ever seen them. And, as I told you earlier, no one has ever gone through the force field and come out alive again.

"I have not had the opportunity of studying one of the Circles at close quarters. There are a great number of them, all apparently identical, each roughly five miles in diameter. Each marks the one-time site of a city. I am assuming that they are dotted over all the land masses of the planet.

"The Toparians are very much afraid of them. They say that if anyone approaches too closely, he loses control of himself and is drawn into the mist, never to be seen again. I have had a chance of viewing one of the Circles from a distance. It was the perfect symmetry of the surrounding mist that led me to suspect it was some form of artificially induced force field. And if that is indeed the case, then the people responsible have developed a technology far in advance of ours on Earth."

"Technology." Lee met my eye. "You don't know the half of it."

"The Toparians have a word for the Circles," said his uncle. "They call them 'Nests.' And they call the people or beings who live in the Nests 'Vorteds.'"

"We saw neither hair nor hide of them," Lee said, and gave a condensed version of our experiences in the artificial woods.

Maver heard him out in silence. He lifted puzzled brows at the description of the apparently very ordinary Earth-type scenery, lifted them still further at the way the branch had moved away from my hand, unfolded his arms and leaned forward when he heard how the tree had dissolved into nothing during the storm.

Then: "Confusing. Little enough to go on." Clasping his huge hands, he rested them in his ragged lap. "Thought-readers, certainly. With the ability to shape matter. But why? Why go to all the trouble of creating an environment to suit your thoughts?"

"It could be curiosity, sir," I said, and offered my theory.

"You could be right, Morton. But even so . . . And

they never showed themselves. That is something I find significant."

He stared down at his hands. "Survival?" he asked them, and now he seemed to be thinking aloud. "And what if there were no survivors? What then? But there is intelligence there . . . In which case the Vorteds could be some new form of life. The product of—"

He broke off, looking up to include us in his reasoning.

"Complete annihilation. The legends are very clear on that score. Everything destroyed. And perhaps the man-made shelters were not deep enough, not as efficient as the deep natural caves of the Toparians' forefathers. So everything vapourised, city and inhabitants alike. And above, a whirling tornado that reached high into the sky. The debris of destruction would be sucked up into the vortex and kept in constant revolving motion for years . . . Animal cells, plant cells, dust. All stirred together in a gigantic test-tube and acted upon by forces beyond our comprehension. Coming together, forming masses, taking on new shapes. And then, as the causative devices lose power, so the tornado loses momentum. The new contents of the vortex gradually sink to the ground. To live there."

"How long ago did all this happen, sir?" I asked.

"Eh?" He regarded me absently. "Oh—hard to say. According to my informant, who gauges time by generations, about two hundred years ago. Four lives, she said, and these people have only short life-spans, an average of fifty years. Legend has it that the Nests were only small at the beginning. But oddly, the mists have always surrounded them, even when they were very small. As the years went by, so the size of the

Nests increased, perhaps directly proportionate to the population they conceal."

He turned to Lee.

"And you have twice been inside one of the Nests. The first time you emerged during a storm. The next time, your escape was part of the hallucination which caused you to relive your passage into this dimension."

"We've long ago given up trying to make any sense of it," Lee said.

"But sense there must be. And something more than idle curiosity, I feel, Morton. We are obviously dealing with intelligent creatures. If creatures they are . . . I would give a great deal to see the inside of one of the Nests for myself."

"Count me out," Lee said laconically. "I've had enough. And I'm damned sure Gerald has too. All I want to do is get back home to Haweford. I'll probably never leave the farm again. My travelling days are over. I've had a bellyful of Toparians, never mind Vorteds. I don't think you'd finished telling us about your heat-ray-toting-friends."

"They are friendly," Maver said earnestly. "I feel certain the ray was only used against you as a warning. They are harmless, and primitive."

"I wouldn't call their weapons harmless," Lee rejoined with some sourness.

"The glass-dart projectors are used only for hunting the animals. If used against a man they would not kill him, only paralyse him. And the heat-rays have been developed primarily for cutting rock with which to build their houses, not as an offensive weapon. There is some similarity to our laser beams. The Toparians' only enemies are the Vorteds, and they discovered long ago that the heat-rays are unable to penetrate or make any impression upon the force fields."

Maver shrugged. "I'm not saying the ray isn't a potentially dangerous weapon. It obviously is. I have had the opportunity of studying one closely. It is simplicity itself. A hollow tube with a reflecting device at one end to trap the sun's rays, an adjustable series of focusing lenses at the other, and a battery of lenses in between. The secret lies in the substance of which the lenses and mirrors are made. In appearance it is similar to our glass, and in fact is obtained from the red sandstone which abounds on this planet. But there the similarity ends. It has vastly different properties from glass, having, among other things, a very high refractive index.

"Although I have actually handled one of the projectors for myself, I have only seen them used at a distance. As far as I am able to judge, the apparatus works by permanently retarding the speed of the concentrated light that passes along the tube. The result is a slow-moving wave front behind which light piles up—folding over on itself, if one can visualise such a process—finally becoming heat.

"They have found many uses for the glass-like substance. They have adapted it to replace the forbidden metals. And for the rest—"

Maver spread his hands in a gesture.

"Life is both hard and precarious for the Toparians. For their staple food they have to rely upon a tasteless creamy mixture made from the fleshy, pulpy top of a small tree that resembles the Earth palm. You must have seen them. The Toparians raise a small grain crop on what little soil there is, and from it make a kind of bread. The rabbit-type animal provides them with clothing and occasional meat. But the flesh is bitter—very much an acquired taste. If there were fish in the seas before the Magnetic War, there are none now. And because of the frequency and violence of the storms, the seas are unusable.

"The Toparians are faced with what seems an insoluble problem. Two problems perhaps, although they are allied. The major one is the provision of food. What little land is arable, is over-worked. And every day the population increases and there are more mouths to be fed.

"The other problem is the long-term one of the Vorted Nests. They are growing steadily, absorbing land. Slow though the process is, one day the Nests inevitably will become linked together. But by then the Toparians will have died of starvation. Unless they can find some way of putting an end to the threat. And with the materials, the technology at their disposal, that is clearly impossible.

"But that day of final extinction of the race lies in the very distant future. It is a menace that troubles only the more far-seeing and intelligent of the Toparians, and they are very few and far between. The others are only concerned with the fact that each square foot of arable land absorbed by the Vorteds is one square foot less on which to grow food."

The Professor fell silent. Lee leaned back, staring sightlessly at the ceiling. After a few minutes I came to my feet and went over to the window. The area in front of the house was still empty, but now it was very obvious by the long shadows thrown across the dusty red tract that the sun was sinking.

Behind me, the room was silent. The Professor had turned in his chair to see what I was doing. I could see his face and Lee's reflected in the glass of the window, Lee's lips pursed in a silent, pensive whistle, Maver's eyes half closed, his craggy forehead deeply furrowed. Each, it seemed, had his own private thoughts to contend with.

As for myself, I felt sympathy for the primitive Toparians. All that the future held for them was slow, inevitable starvation. The Toparians had given us a rough time out there on the hill, but before that they had shared their food with us. They could quite easily have let us grow hungry. A kindly people . . . with stolid, dull-looking faces that rarely seemed to show expression. "The farsighted and intelligent of them," Maver had said, "are few and far between." Meaning that the average Toparian was content to exist from day to day without any thought for the future, without any regard for the scarcity of food. Feeding us would have meant no sacrifice to people like that. They would have given us food automatically, as we would have fed a stray dog.

And the few that were more intelligent than the rest were presumably the leaders. Maver had said that Adam Sokel—never having met the man I found it easy to think of him as a Toparian—had been a person of some importance in his own country.

And then I remembered something and, pursuing that memory, came up with other things too—things the Professor had told us. And they slotted together to form a picture that turned my blood to ice.

Ready to voice my fears I swung to face the room. In the same moment Maver sat up quickly and addressed a question to Lee, his voice sharp with urgency.

"When you first arrived—when you were on the hill. Can you be absolutely certain that you were not moved—not taken inside the Nest?"

"We're sure," Lee said. "There was proof. A stone, a patch of grass—" And he would have gone on to enlarge upon the proof, but his uncle was talking again.

"The Vorteds must have extended their screen to enclose you. This is something the Toparians don't know about, or if they do, my informant didn't mention it. A new facet . . . The Vorteds are able to alter the shape of their boundaries. Under general conditions they obviously maintain the figure of a circle because that is the most efficient shape for their purpose, the one that encloses the largest area of land. The Nests are growing, but only slowly. They are clearly unable to enlarge their boundaries at will. But if the need arises they can change their shapes, drawing in the screen at one sector, extending it at another."

"Flexible," Lee said. "That's probably what happened. They stretched out and took us in."

"They captured you as they would any other potential victims who ventured within reach," Maver said in a flat tone. "But then they read in your minds that you were something very different from the usual victims. They discovered you had come from another world. To enable them to suck as much information from your minds as possible they created surroundings which they assumed would make you relax and feel at ease. Where there is no tension, thoughts come easily and smoothly. They learned that you had come from a world of rich lands, a civilized world free of the constant magnetic storms of this.

"There is one factor I had overlooked, although it was staring me in the face. The Toparians have their problem of growing population and dwindling food. The Vorteds must have the same problem. Only, restricted as they are by their boundaries, their problem must be even more acute. Do you understand what I am trying to say?"

For a moment or two it was clear that Lee didn't. But I did, and horror flowed over me like a tide.

"It was curiosity," I said with an effort. "But not idle curiosity. They had a reason."

"They had a reason for picking your brains," Maver said. "They made you relive your entry into this dimension so that they could discover the means you used. Now they know how you did it and where the field is. And they will know that you are expecting the field to come back again. And when it does—"

Lee understood now. His voice was the same grey monotone as his uncle's.

"They will reach out to enclose it," he said. "Then they will go through the door when it opens. They will try to invade Earth."

CHAPTER TWELVE

Professor Maver made it all very clear.

"They will withdraw the screens on two perimeters. The circle will become first an ellipse, then a narrow strip. The strip will reach out to enclose the area where the door is due to appear. And when it does—"

He broke off.

And I had two fears to contend with, the one I had worked out for myself and which was still unvoiced, and now this second one, infinitely more horrifying.

"Is there nothing we can do about it?" I asked. And knew before the words were out how stupid the question had been.

Maver ignored me.

"If only we knew something about them," he said. "So many questions without answers. Why, when they are intelligent enough to develop a force field, are they unable to enlarge their territory at will? Why, when they had you in their power, did they choose to remain out of sight? Unless they didn't want to alarm you by their appearance . . . That might be the answer."

Lee said, "I thought once that they might be invisible."

"Invisible?" The Professor shook his head. "No, Lee. I don't think so for one moment. Don't let your imagination run riot. Use the few facts we know when making your guesses. We know they must be made of the matter of destruction of the Magnetic War. Vapourised fluids, including blood. Vegetable and animal cells. Dust. The plant life of this world, the little that has survived, is very similar to plant life on Earth. Even without the proof of a microscope I am certain the cellular make-up will be the same. The common or garden cell enclosed in a cellulose wall. The nucleus set in cytoplasm. A very ordinary carbohydrate cell, the inevitable product of conditions that are the same here as on Earth.

"Animal life here is much like that which we have in our world. The cells will certainly be similar. Whatever form of life exists now inside the Nests will be solid. But I cannot envisage what that life may be like in appearance. Perhaps wholly animal, perhaps wholly vegetable. Perhaps a little of each. And then, too, the dust . . . Sandstone dust. Silica . . ."

My mind filled with pictures, terrifying pictures. I turned to look through the window again.

"If only it were possible to get into one of the Nests," came the Professor's voice. "To examine, to investigate. Learn from the surroundings, even if those surroundings are artifical. There must be clues . . ."

The shadows had lengthened appreciably since the last time I had looked outside. Dusk couldn't be far

away. There could be little of the Professor's two
hours left to go. I had best stay at the window to
watch for whoever would bring the evening meal.
Lee and I could hide in one of the other rooms. And
afterwards?

"We can't just sit here like this—doing nothing!"
That was Lee, his voice bursting out harsh, almost
unrecognisable.

And then: "Adam. He can help us. God knows
you did him a favor, making it possible for him to
get back home. He owes you that much. You can
speak the lingo, Uncle John. When they bring the
food, talk to them. Make them see it's urgent we see
Adam."

"No!" I spoke involuntarily, sharply, before Maver
had a chance to reply. I turned to face them again.
"It's no use asking Adam for help, Lee."

"Why the hell not?" he demanded. "Just because
he's kept out of the way? That's plain damned stupid!"

"Not that." I shook my head. "Something else." It
was time to tell them of the conclusion I had reached
before the Professor dropped his bombshell. But
where to start?

"Remember Wembley Stadium?" I asked Lee.

He gaped. "What about it?"

Maver looked from my face to Lee's. "I don't understand—"

"Portable," I said quickly. "Made to stand on a
slope. Ladders leading up to the platform on top.
Platform about five feet from the ground." I paused
fractionally. "Which is just about the height of the
door from the top of the hill. And the ground below
slopes."

For a moment Lee was puzzled. Then understand-
ing came and exploded on his face.

"Not the Toparians too?" he gasped incredulously.

"Everything points to it. There was that heavily-armed party we saw waiting nearby. There's the fact that Adam didn't see fit to tell your uncle that the door had reappeared and that we'd come through. He must have known about us, even if the door wasn't spotted. The fact that—"

"What's all this about?" Maver broke in brusquely, almost angrily.

Lee told him briefly about the wooden contraption we had come across in the hollow near our hill. That, in itself, was convincing enough.

The Professor came to his feet.

"That explains the unusual activity here today," he said. "Men from other villages, strangers, all carrying weapons; some passing through, others staying, settling themselves out of sight in the houses . . ."

Lee, being who he was, indulged in a flash of wry humour.

"Aliens queuing up to invade Earth," said he. "Three starters—including our little party. And who are the favorites?"

Maver held up his hand. "Quiet. Let me think."

"We've got to get out of here," I said.

The ugly face looked absently at me. "Yes."

"The Vorteds are already within reach of the door —only a stone's throw away. So are the Toparians. We must get out there too."

"Yes," Maver agreed again. And then, almost pathetically. "I liked Adam. I always trusted him."

"They'll soon be here with the evening meal," I said.

"Eh?" He seemed unable to cope with his thoughts. "Yes. Very soon."

I turned back to keep watch.

"The Vorteds are the greatest threat," Lee said behind me. "The unknown quantity. What they're capable of—what sort of weapons they'll have . . . At least we know almost everything there is to know about the Toparians. Except how many of them there are."

"This is an average settlement," came Mayer's heavy reply. "Population—oh, five hundred, over half of them men. There is no great distance between any of the villages so far as I know. There must be scores, hundreds within marching distance. It's obvious men are already coming in from outlying districts. They're massing. And most of those I've seen were carrying heat-projectors."

"That's what I was thinking of," Lee said. "Tanks wouldn't stand a chance. In any case, they'd be well established before tanks could be brought up. Infantry would be massacred. How far can those damned heat-rays reach?"

"In theory," Maver said, "to infinity."

"We'd have to use atomic weapons against them. Drop an atomic bomb smack in their middle. That'd stir things up. No . . . They'd be able to bring the plane down before it got anywhere near."

"Surmise of that kind is only a waste of time."

But Lee pursued his theme.

"Missiles then. If they could be brought to bear before the rays got to them." An idea occurred to him and he became excited. "Light . . . You say the projectors work by reflecting sunlight. That means they can't be used at night or when there's no sun."

"The light source need not be the sun," Maver said. "Any source will serve, no matter how faint. The light is collected inside the tube until it is powerful enough to form the beam. The fainter the source, the longer it takes to bring the weapon into use. That's all. Even a lighted match, if it could burn long enough, would be sufficient."

I was impatient at an interchange that seemed to

be a waste of time. But there was nothing we could do until the evening meal was brought.

"Does only one of them come with the food?" I asked without taking my eyes from the twilight space outside.

"Two," Maver replied. "One with the food, the other with water for the bathroom."

"How do they carry the water?"

"In bags made of animal hide."

"Two of them, Lee." I watched his reflection in the glass.

"We'll cope," said he, and I was able to see his nod of assurance. "One each side the door, yes? We could use some kind of help—" He looked about him.

"Home-made coshes." I dug my foot into the packed earth and dust of the floor, loosened it and scraped a pile together. "Socks filled with this."

"Even when we shared the same digs," Lee said, "you were always a great one for improvisation." While he busied himself removing his shoes and socks, I excavated more filling, without taking my eyes from the window. Crouching at my feet he filled the sandbags.

"No need for a ceiling break-out this time," he grunted. "We wait until it's really dark and then leave in style by the front door. Right?"

"Right," I agreed, and Maver said shortly: "No. We can't move in darkness. It would be suicide."

"Suicide?" Frowning, Lee straightened, a dirt-packed sock in each hand. "Why?"

"That should be obvious, Lee. Even the Topari-ans are too afraid to leave the village at night, and they know all the places of shelter out there."

"You mean because of the storms?"

"Today has been a quiet day. There's been only the one storm, and that was a comparatively mild one. At night, when the sky is dark, there is little or no indication that one is on its way. They break almost without warning. And to be caught in the open during a bad one means death—a very unpleasant death."

"What about the moons and the stars?" Lee asked. "Can't we keep an eye on those? Surely they'll give some kind of warning."

I left them to thrash it out.

Maver had another reason for not moving by night.

"We would have to make for the hills. And up there we would be faced with the hazard of the paralysing bushes."

"We'll just have to take the risk," Lee said flatly. "One thing's for sure—we've got to get back to our hill and we can't wait for daylight. We wouldn't stand an earthly chance of getting away."

His reflected, raised brows invited my agreement. I nodded—very reluctantly—but I nodded. "We'll have to take our chances with both storms and spines. There's no alternative."

"There's no question of chancing the storms," Maver said grimly. "There's been at least one every night all the months I have been here. Don't be misled by the one you experienced today. That was little more than a stiff blow."

He went across the room to rest one hand on the wall.

"Have you noticed how they build their houses with sloping walls? That's to obviate the risk of being blown down. Have you seen how thick the walls are? Two feet and more. Solidly constructed. And I have known times when the whole house shook as if it were made of reeds. The roofs, flat to offer no resistance, pliable to give with the force, are still often swept bodily away.

"You must understand the nature of these storms. They are the direct result of the Magnetic War, caused by the distortion to the natural magnetic fields. A long time ago the storms were much more frequent and destructive. As time goes by, so their intensity decreases. One day, in the remote future, there will be an end to them. But now they are something we have to take into account. A man could not stay alive in a bad one. The combination of the magnetic surge and driving dust would flay the flesh from his bones."

"You conjure up a pretty picture," Lee observed dryly.

"No more than the truth," rejoined his uncle simply. And then, after all his attempts at dissuasion—or perhaps he had not meant his earlier rejection of our plan to move during darkness, perhaps he had not been trying to make us change our minds but had only wanted us to be sure we knew the danger involved—after all that long discussion he said, "But you are right, of course. If we are to leave here, it will have to be under cover of darkness. All we can do is provide ourselves with food and water—and then make for the hills with all possible speed in the hope of finding adequate shelter in time."

And now it was dark. Burning scarlet and blazing gold streaked the horizon sky. The moons had not yet risen, but overhead unfamiliar patterns of stars twinkled. I looked down from them to find the area in front of the house empty no longer.

"They're coming," I warned.

CHAPTER THIRTEEN

Twilight seemed to last a long time in this dimension. Although the sun had set and the stars were out, there was still enough light left for us to see what we were doing.

We stood, one each side of the door, with our backs against the wall.

"You'd better take the far side," Lee had suggested only half jocularly. "Being left-handed you'll get a better crack at them from that side."

I found reassurance in the feel and weight of my improvised cosh.

"Let 'em get inside first," Lee whispered. "I'll slam the door behind. One of 'em may try to make a bolt for it." He essayed an experimental swing with his sandbag. "The back of the neck, I think . . ."

Sandals slithered softly on the hard ground outside. I poised my weapon as the door started to open.

The details of what happened then were lost in the half-light and the confusion. I was aware of two fur-clad figures, one carrying a bowl and a small basket, the other with shoulders bent by the weight of two leather bags. Two slow-motion silhouettes . . . Then the door slammed and I stepped forward. My home-made cosh, swinging, thudded down across the neck of the nearest Toparian. He reeled forward, bowl and basket flying from his grasp, and dropped to his knees, then his face. As I threw myself down on him, my knees jammed into the small of his back. Letting my sandbag fall so that I could grip his neck with one hand, I clamped the other over his mouth in case he was still conscious and able to shout.

It was an unnecessary precaution; he was out cold. Breathing heavily, heart thumping, I leaned back to look at Lee. Still on his feet, he was looking down at his prone victim with every expression of a job well done.

Lee grinned at me, but his voice was inclined to shake a little.

"Easier than I imagined. I must take this sort of thing up as a hobby. The satisfaction . . ."

Maver moved quickly to retrieve the two precious water-containers, both lying sideways on the floor, one leaking a little. He propped them against the wall, then stepped over the white mush contents of the bowl that had splattered across the floor to open the door a fraction while he peered out into the semi-darkness. Closing it, he nodded confirmation that all was well outside, then busied himself collecting the small loaves that had scattered from the basket.

To immobilise my victim I sacrificed strips from the tail of my shirt. Gagging him, I bound his wrists together behind his back and then used his own cord belt to tie his ankles. As Lee had said, there was a queer sort of satisfaction to be derived from

the affair. He dealt with his Toparian in much the
same way. When both our prisoners were securely
trussed, he set about emptying his socks and replacing them on his feet.

We stuffed our pockets with the loaves of bread.
Lee picked up one of the water-bags, I the other. The
Professor opened the door again for another survey
outside. It was really dark now. Both the Toparians
had regained consciousness, and their eyes glistened
whitely as they followed our movements. We
dragged them to the wall, propped them up and
made them as comfortable as we could. I seemed to
remember muttering some kind of apology; they
looked so helpless and harmless. From his post at the
door Maver nodded impatiently. We left the house
for all the world as if we were doing a moonlight
flit without paying the rent.

The sky was high and clear, ablaze with the strange
constellations of stars. The twin moons had yet to
appear, but even without them there was more than
enough light for us to see the way. We went round
the side of the house and paused in the shadows
there for one last final inspection. We had a fairly
good view of the village. Nothing moved, everywhere
was quiet, and there were no lights in any of the windows. It was like a village of the dead.

We had no trouble in reaching the belt of palm
trees. If anything—if one could have forgotten what
lay behind all this—it was almost a pleasant evening
stroll. But it was already obvious, even at that early
stage, that we would not be able to keep up our rate
of progress. For one thing, the bags we carried were
much more heavy and cumbersome than we had bar-
gained for. Each held perhaps the equivalent of
three buckets of water; they were no light weight.
Neither were they provided with handles.

The other impediment was much more serious,

something neither Lee nor I—nor the Professor—had taken into account. Both Lee and I had noticed Maver's bare feet when we had first met him, but after that we had just taken them for granted, forgetting all about them. As had their owner.

Inspecting them, he admitted as much.

"I've got used to pottering about the village like this—the ground's not very rough between the houses. I was only wearing thin canvas shoes when I came through the field, and they wore out very quickly. The Toparians supplied me with a pair of their sandays, but I found them most cramping and uncomfortable. I wore them very little . . ."

"We'd best go back for them," Lee said doubtfully.

"I don't even know where they are." His uncle looked up worriedly at the sky. "We cannot afford the time."

"We can't afford to have your feet slashed to ribbons," Lee rejoined sensibly, and looked about him. "We might be able to find some kind of substitute."

We did. We used palm leaves folded and tied about the Professor's feet with more strips from our shirts. The result was a fairly serviceable and moderately comfortable pair of makeshift moccasins. And while we worked, Mayer's eyes were continually turned to the sky, his worried voice urging us to hurry . . . When we set off again, moving now across the lower, gentle slopes, he kept pace with us well, even at times forging ahead in his haste to be away from the village and in sight of shelter.

His anxiety increased as the steeper slope and tumbled rock perforce slowed us down. My back and shoulders were already aching with the weight of the water-bag which I had to keep changing from hand to hand Lee, I noted, was having to do the same.

After a while, when we were some distance from the village, the twin moons rose, their orbs flooding the landscape with a clear yellow light. But only for a short while. Five minutes or so later the light was wiped away as if a curtain had been drawn. So unexpectedly that, about to climb a rocky funnel between sharp-edged pinnacles, we stopped and turned with surprise. And because Lee and I had seen once before the ominous coiling in the sky that was the prelude to a storm, we didn't need the Professor's warning to make us quicken our pace. We scrambled along as fast as we were able.

There was the same change to the air we had experienced before, the same nettle-rash tingling on the exposed flesh of face and hands. There was the stirring of the breeze, the first indication of the coming of the oppressive heat. Gradually the stars winked out. The breeze strengthened, lifting clouds of dust before it, invisible clouds, but stinging against the sides of our faces. As the light faded, so we had to slacken our pace. Now we had the hazard of the spined shrubs to contend with. It was no longer safe to grope blindly for handholds. Not knowing if our trousers would be sufficient protection against the spines, we had to peer ahead before taking each step, making all the use we could of what little light still remained.

And with each step I took, the water-bag became heavier. I tried carrying it slung over one shoulder, but that was no better; its weight digging through the thin fabric of my shirt chafed the flesh beneath.

An unexpected, vicious gust drove us against the wall of a ravine. In the silence that followed I could hear the breath sobbing in Maver's throat. I wondered how long it would be before he would have to give up. Lee and I were young; he was an old man. We rested there, leaning against the warm rock.

And then we heard the distant roaring. The sound set us moving again. Another gust drove us back. We fought against it, struggled forward to be met by an even fiercer gust as we emerged from the ravine. There was still enough light left for me to see Lee take hold of his uncle's shoulder to steady the old man against the rising fury. To help, I put the flat of my free hand between Maver's shoulder-blades, and between us we managed to struggle on against a wind that now seemed to be coming from all directions at once, tingling, biting with dust, stinging hands and faces.

With the wind rising to a shrieking inferno we fought our way round a corner to come up against what at first seemed to be a solid unbroken wall of rock.

It was Lee who found the narrow entrance to the cave. Finding it was the result of good luck and not management. The wind hurled him against the wall —hurled us all, separating us—and sent him rolling along it. Then Lee vanished. And reappeared, beckoning. His mouth—a dark circle on shapeless white—was open in a shout that was lost in the tumult. But his meaning was clear.

We were just able to make out the black slit of the cleft. We staggered the last few feet towards it, my free arm about Maver's shoulders, Lee reaching to help. The storm broke in its full fury as we turned the corner into safety.

I spent my first night in Dimension A huddled with the others in the pitch blackness at the far end of a cave that could only have been a few feet wide and perhaps a score of yards deep.

While the storm lasted, life—to say the least—was unpleasant. The wind lashed into the cave, driving dust with it. The thundering, deafening roar seemed to reach inside my head, where a numbness precluded thought and reason. We crouched with our backs towards the cave entrance. Hands covering our faces, we protected them as best we could against the dust and magnetic tingle. There were times when I was sure I could feel the ground rocking under my knees. Once, even above the tumult, I heard a crash, as if a rock had been hurled against the cave opening.

It lasted a lifetime, that unbelievable storm. And then came the time when the roar seemed not quite so loud, when there seemed to be breaks in the wind, so that now it came in gusts. Gradually the intervals between the gusts lengthened. Gradually, imperceptibly, there was a diminishing of the howling, shrieking inferno. For a while, wind still lashed into our shelter. Then that too ceased. The night was silent and still. Uncovering my face, I opened my eyes. Light, the pale golden radiance of the moons, was already filtering into the cave.

Lee was stretching himself, looking back fearfully over his shoulder as if unable to believe it was all over. And the Professor—astonishingly, he was asleep, head ledged against jutting rock, mouth drooping open. But then, after his long stay in this world, he must have become accustomed to the magnetic storms, able to sleep through them.

Recovered, Lee regarded his uncle and then turned to grin at me with eyebrows raised. Still without speaking he licked his lips and nodded at the water-bags propped against my side. I heaved one over to him. He needed a few fumbling moments to master the thongs that bound its neck. And then he had to struggle to raise the water-bag to his mouth. When he finished he passed it back to me, and it was my turn to cope with its weight and awkward shape. More water spilled down my chest than passed my lips. I hadn't realised just how parched I had become.

Carefully refastening the thongs, I set the bag upright against the wall.

Lee said softly, "That was a snorter and no mistake. Worse than that other one. Now I see what Uncle John was driving at. If we hadn't found this place in time—" His shudder was graphic. "What a hell of a world in which to live."

"You can't really blame the Toparians for trying to find somewhere else," I said.

"To blazes with that! This is their bed, they made it, now they've got to lie on it. One day there'll be an end to the storms. In the meantime they've learnt to live with them. They've got the Vorted Nests to contend with. All right, so what about our Iron Curtain? They're finding food tightish. I'll warrant they're still better provided for than a few million people in our world. It's up to them to sort their problems out without trying to overflow in our direction."

His voice had risen toward the latter part of the diatribe. I glanced warningly at the sleeping Professor.

"If he could sleep through that lot . . . ," Lee said. And then: "Yes." He closed his eyes. I leaned against the wall and closed my eyes as well. Sleep must have come almost immediately. I woke only once during the night, when a sound disturbed me. At first I thought another storm must be blowing up, but it turned out to be the steady drumming of heavy rain.

When I awoke the next time, I found the cave flooded with the clear light of morning.

The professor was still asleep, but Lee—awake and about—was standing at the entrance. Coming stiffly to my feet I went to join him. He moved to one side so that I could see outside. There were pools of water in the hollows of the narrow rock ledge that fronted the cave. Beyond was a sea of drifting white mist. It was almost like looking from a plane onto a bank of clouds.

"Came the dawn," he said. "Sleep well?"

"The rain woke me once."

"Me too. It must have been quite a downpour. I've been up some time." Hands in his pockets, he leaned against the side of the entrance. "Doing some thinking. We've been in this damned place a little over twenty-four hours. Back on Earth that's only a couple of hours. Almost impossible to imagine, isn't it? I wonder how long it was before Leming found we were missing?"

"I've thought about that too," I told him. "It was a bit after six-thirty when I came over to the lab. Mrs. Robson was in the kitchen, so she'd know where I'd gone. She'd have breakfast ready for about half past seven. I'm guessing she'd do as she'd done before— give the lab a ring to let me know the meal was ready."

Lee took over the process of reasoning.

"Getting no reply, what would she do? Come over to the lab herself? Almost a certainty. You didn't lock the door behind you, Gerald?"

It seemed an age ago since I had pushed the metal door open and gone into the lab.

"No. This time they won't have to waste time breaking it open. Which probably means Mr. Leming will know by eight o'clock that something is wrong. Which means too that right now he's only had about half an hour in which to try to get the field back again. Not very long."

"That's how I had it figured," Lee said soberly. "As you say, not very long. Barely time to get the sleep out of his eyes. And we don't know whether the equipment was damaged or not. According to Uncle John, it probably was. So it will have to be repaired again before Leming can even start trying to find the right sequence of readings. And every hour back there is almost a dany and a night here."

He brooded on that for a while and then turned to glance back over his shoulder into the cave as if to reassure himself that his uncle was still sleeping.

"There's something else I've been mulling over," he continued in a low voice. "Dabbling in the possible future, envisaging a situation that might arise. We're on our way now to the hill to be ready there for when the door opens. The Vorteds and the Toparians are already there, presumably with the same idea in mind. Suppose . . ."

He paused.

"Suppose we got there safely and saw the door open, but knew we didn't stand a chance of getting through it. That could happen. And suppose we could see either the Vorteds or the Toparians making preparations to go through. And suppose again that we had the means of destroying the door before they could get to it. Would we destroy it, knowing that as a result we would probably be marooned in this place for the rest of our lives?"

It was an unusual, serious mood for Lee. And an unusual grim mask for his face.

He pressed the thing home, making sure I understood.

"At the risk of sounding corny, would we be prepared to sacrifice ourselves for the sake of mankind?"

He had envisaged a situation that I had not thought about before, a situation that might easily happen, and one which I was coward enough not to want to dwell on now. There was a way of evading his question.

"Even if we want to, we haven't the means of destroying the door."

"We would have if we could lay our hands on one of those heat-projectors. All we would have to do

then is point it at the door, directing the ray through
it. It would play havoc with that equipment in the
lab, putting it out of action, probably for good. I'm
damned sure no one would know enough about the
equipment to be able to rebuild it."

"If the door was open," I said bleakly, "Leming
would be in the lab."

"He would. That would make four of us." Lee
stared down at the cotton wool mist. "In a way, he'd
be better off than we three left here. He'd be dead."

His cold, dispassionate voice shook me. I fought
anger.

"That's all surmise. It may not happen like that at
all. And even if it did—we couldn't kill—"

And a voice came in from behind.

"We would have to, Morton. I know Martin Leming. If he knew—if it were possible for the choice to
be laid in front of him, I know which he would take."

Lee turned to regard his uncle.

"So do we try to get hold of one of those projectors?" he asked.

The other nodded. "Yes, I think so. Even if only as
a precautionary measure. You have put into words
an idea I have been harbouring for some time. Let us
hope that Morton is right, that the contingency will
not arise. But there is a strong possibility it will."

He pushed between us to step out into the open,
looking about him. The warmth of the sun was dis-
pelling the mists to some small extent. Through a gap
on the right we caught a glimpse of the village, much
nearer than I had imagined. In the few seconds before the mist closed in, we could see signs of great
activity down there, much coming and going of
armed Toparians.

"They'll know by now we've slipped out of their
clutches," Lee observed unnecessarily.

"All that activity won't be for our benefit," Maver

said. "They've something more important on their minds. But I think they will make an effort to find us. Helpless though they must know we are, we still constitute something of a hazard."

Rubbing the overnight stubble on his chin he moved to stand at the rim of the ledge, looking towards the left, the route we would have to take to reach our hill. The mists were clearing more rapidly in that direction. Through ragged gaps we could see glimpses of the lowlands, but the hollows were still filled with dense whiteness.

Lee produced a flattened loaf from his pocket, broke it, and bit on the crust.

"A sketchy breakfast," he mumbled through a full mouth, "and then we hit the trail again. Get moving while we've still got that stuff to hide us."

But his uncle wasn't sure that this was such a good idea. The mist would afford cover, he conceded, but it would also hide the spined shrubs. Making my own frugal meal of bread and water, I left them to their weighing up of the pros and cons, and was thankful later that I wasn't called upon to make the casting vote. Lee, unaided, was able to persuade Maver that the advantage of the mist outweighed its disadvantage. The mist, clearing again on the right, revealed the village and its activity, a sight that put the finishing touch to his persuasions. If we could see the Toparians, then it would be only a matter of time before they spotted us. Withdrawing ourselves and our still-more-or-less-white shirts into the cave, we made final preparations for the move, such as they were— merely a matter of finishing off the bread and each having a drink of water, Lee holding one of the bags while his uncle drank.

A quick glance outside showed that the village was hidden again. But it was obvious by the dissolving tendrils that it would not remain so for long. We left our cave to make our way as quickly as we could along the ledge, trying to put as much distance as possible between ourselves and the village while the mists persisted. Lee took the lead, carefully avoiding mist-pooled hollows which might contain shrubs. From time to time we could catch the sound of distant voices. Oddly, they seemed to come from all directions. We rounded an elbow of rock and Lee came to a halt, dropping to his knees, motioning for us to do the same. There were no drifting clouds here to hide the scene. We could see how the lower slopes and the flatlands beyond were alive with moving figures.

Not a dozen yards below us a line of six Toparians, all bearing heat-projectors, toiled along a path that ran parallel to the way we had been going. So close were they that if we had spoken they would certainly have heard. I looked back. Behind them, a little lower down, another armed party was climbing the slope at an angle. On a still lower level was a third group. I looked back then towards the cave. It was still in sight, almost hidden by the rock projection, but I could see the ledge and the Toparians who clustered there.

"Looks like we moved off just in time," Lee whispered softly, small triumph in his voice at this vindication of his earlier persuasions.

"We're not out of the woods yet," I whispered back.

Certainly, we could not stay put—the climbing party was headed straight in our direction. At least the way ahead seemed clear, just as long as the file below didn't change its mind and start to climb. I didn't think they would. I had the feeling that this activity was an organised search, that each level of the slopes was being systematically combed.

Maver worriedly rubbed the overnight stubble on his craggy chin.

"I recognise none of the faces," he said in an undertone. "Strangers . . . And obviously well organised. A new departure for these people."

The same thought occurred to Lee and me at the same time. He put it into words while I was seeking tactful phraseology.

"You don't think this could be Adam's hand at work?"

"It is a possibility," Maver said. "And if he is responsible, then it would appear he has profited by his stay in our world."

The party below had moved out of sight, hidden now by a series of jagged pieces of rock, their shape that of the spiked back of a mythical dragon. We took the opportunity to make our own move, crouching, working our way along the ledge. But as ledges have a habit of doing, it petered out, leaving us with no alternative but to drop to a lower level. And that new level was a hollow filled with mist. A steep gully —a kind of fireman's chute—led towards it, and Lee, heedless of his uncle's muttered warning, went slithering down. The bottom of the gully itself was clear, and so Lee was safe enough from the danger of the spines. As I was preparing to follow, lowering my legs over the brink, Lee moved away, his legs becoming swallowed by the mist. I slid down, more clumsily than Lee had done, dropping sideways when I hit the bottom. His sudden exclamation I took at first to be the result of my awkward descent. But it wasn't. He stopped, bent double, then came stumbling back towards me, falling to the ground as I came to my feet. He had his hand clamped tightly about his ankle, and I knew, with a cold thrill of fear, what must have happened.

"Like a needle," he said, and even tried to grin. "My leg's gone to sleep."

The professor, his face filled with concern, looked down at us from the top of the chute.

"It doesn't hurt." Lee massaged his ankle. "Just nothing—dead. Just as if . . ."

And then his voice trailed away, his eyes closed, and he slumped back.

I knelt at his side. He was unconscious. I looked back up at the Professor and he nodded reassurance of a kind.

"Nothing permanent. I have seen this happen before. There's no lasting effect. But it will be some time before he regains consciousness."

Filled with relief, at least on that score, I turned to look at the hollow. The mist filled the bottom completely. It would be foolish to go through the mist, impossible to go round. I turned back to look up at Maver, and I didn't have to say anything. He had lowered himself to his stomach and was leaning out over the top of the narrow gully, his reaching hands beckoning.

It was going to be no easy job getting Lee's unconscious body back up again. I dragged him into a sitting position, his head lolling on his chest like that of a sawdust-filled marionette, and then I lifted him as best I could until he was lying backwards in the gully. After that it was a matter of pushing him up an inch at a time, steadying him, until Maver was able to grasp his shoulders. Between us we managed it. The Professor reached down again, this time for my benefit. I scrabbled my way up and then flopped to the ground, not enough strength left even to get to my feet.

I think I knew then our position was hopeless. With Lee the way he was, it would be impossible to carry on. Our only hope—and a faint one at that— was that we might be able to find some nearby place of concealment where we could wait until Lee recovered.

I managed to come to my knees. Ahead, the ledge narrowed until it became impassable. The rocky wall behind us towered smoothly upwards without a single break in its red surface. I looked back the way we had come. Not a dozen yards away one of the lines of Toparians was coming towards us. Our recapture was as inglorious as that—as ignominious as the first time when we had been caught with figurative pants down.

The Professor clasped his hands in a wry gesture of resignment. I remember wondering whether I ought to climb to my feet with my hands over my head in the approved fashion. But maybe our Earth-style type of surrender would have no meaning for these people. And I remember thinking too, in the few seconds it took them to reach us, that when they had made prisoners of us this time they would take damned good care we didn't escape again. Any hope of ever reaching our hill and the door was finally, irrevocably squashed.

CHAPTER FOURTEEN

There was nothing gentle about our capture this time. One of the Toparians, a scowling, burly type with the unusual adornment of a beard, grabbed my shoulder roughly, hauled me to my feet and then jerked his heat-projector at Lee's unconscious body in an unmistakable command. I stooped to set my hands under the limp shoulders. Maver took hold of the feet. There were a few moments of delay while one of the Toparians slid efficiently down the gully to retrieve the two water-bags we had dropped in the hollow. Shouts were exchanged, and the parties that had been scouring the slopes started to make their way back to the level ground.

Burdened as Maver and I were, it was a long, slow journey back to the village. A journey, for my part, made all the more uncomfortable and miserable by the knowledge of our hopeless position, by wonder-

ing what the future held in store for us now, and by
the continual jabbing of a projector in my back as
the bearded Toparian at my heels tried to make me
move faster. I really came to hate that particular gentleman. It was a relief when we finally emerged from
the palm plantation that fringed the settlement. Having been given no opportunity of resting, of lowering
the dead weight of my load to the ground, my arms
felt as if they were being pulled from their sockets.
By the way the Professor was staggering, he was in
worse shape than I was.

I was a little surprised to be marched back to the
same house we had left not all that long ago. Ungen-
tle hands thrust us inside. The door was slammed violently behind. We lowered Lee to the ground, and
while I dragged him to the wall so that I could prop
him against it, Maver flopped down on the chair,
closing his eyes.

Lee showed no signs of regaining consciousness.
He had been out for quite some time now. Rubbing
his hands, even slapping his cheeks, produced no result. I sat back on my heels and looked at Maver,
worry making me unreasonably angry with his closed
eyes and slumped posture.

"How long?" I asked sharply.

"Eh?" He opened his eyes.

"How long does it take this damned stuff to wear
off?"

"Varies," he replied wearily. "So I'm told." He
shook himself into full awareness. "I suppose it de-
pends upon the depth of penetration, how much of
the sap has been released into his blood stream. His
trousers will have protected him to some extent. Don't
worry, Morton. He should be recovering soon. When
he does, he will probably feel rather ill."

But I felt I couldn't, just couldn't stand round and
wait; I had to do something, anything . . .

"Water," I said, and went quickly to the bathroom, there to soak my handkerchief in the contents of the glass ewer. When I returned, Maver was kneeling at Lee's side. He looked up. "Pulse strong enough. He's all right."

I dabbed the impassive features. When that produced no effect I squeezed the handkerchief over his face, letting the water splash over him.

Lee stirred and opened his eyes, blinking up at the ceiling. His gaze travelled down the wall, touched on the window, passed across the table, and came to rest on my face.

His smile was a ghost. "Home, sweet home," he said. The ghost-smile faded. "Hell," he whispered, and closed his eyes again.

"How are you feeling, Lee?" Maver asked.

"Groggy." Lee opened his eyes again so that he could do full justice to his grimace of discomfort. "Decidedly off-colour. Those things must pack a punch like the kick of a mule."

He leaned forward to massage his legs.

"Feeling coming back." He looked past me at his uncle. "Sorry about getting us all in trouble again." His gaze came back to me. "Another round-up. Did I miss anything, Gerald?"

"No excitement. They came, they saw, and they frogmarched us away."

"So we're—"

He broke off as the door crashed open. I sprang to my feet. Maver seemed too weary to show any reaction.

Two armed Toparians stood arrogantly in the doorway. Between their shaggy heads I could see two more waiting outside. Ignoring Lee and me, the first two marched towards Maver and grasping his arms, made it very clear that he was to accompany them. He obeyed with a kind of couldn't-care-less resignation. The door slammed behind them, and I went quickly to the window to watch them marching him away. They marched with almost military precision, one in front, one on either side, one behind, projector tubes carried at a precise angle. A firing squad escorting their victim to the place of execution. I found the sight disturbing to say the least. I craned to look sideways. Three men were on duty outside the door.

"What's going on?" Lee cried behind me. He was trying to struggle to his feet. I went to help.

"What have they done with him?" he asked.

I nodded backwards. "They've taken him towards the centre of the village."

"Why take only him?"

"No doubt we'll find out in due course," I said with more calmness than I was feeling.

"If they do anything to him—" he said through his teeth, and left the rest unspoken, perhaps conscious of the futility of any threat he could make.

"Can you walk?" I asked him then.

Lee tried a couple of lurching steps. "More or less. Still numb, like treading on wool." He shook himself free from my help. "I'll manage . . ."

There was no point in discussing our predicament, in trying to figure out what they intended doing with the Professor. Picking up my soaked handkerchief I took it to the bathroom to rinse it out in the ewer, mainly for something to do. The mirror showed me a face of streaked grime, fiery red skin, and unkempt hair that was barely recognisable. The day-old beard didn't help the picture any. I would have given a lot for a comb and a razor. The Professor, beardless, must have had access to some kind of razor. I searched but found nothing. It seemed the Toparians didn't believe in leaving potential weapons about the place.

I stripped to the waist and plunged my face into

the bowl, flooding off as much dirt as I could, afterwards dabbing myself dry with a handful of leaves. As I reached for my shirt there came the sound of the outer door being opened and closed. I went hurriedly back to the main room.

The Professor was back—and what relief there was at the sight of him, standing by the table, staring down at it, one hand absently playing with the cord about his waist. He looked very old and very tired.

Lee limped awkwardly to his side, made to speak, and then thought better of it. Maver was silent for a while. Then he sighed heavily, straightened his shoulders and spoke to a point somewhere between us.

"Adam—" he said in a quiet, strained voice. "They took me to Adam. In one of the houses . . . The place was fitted up like—like a battle headquarters. He's changed . . . I was right—he has learned from his stay on our world. A dictator—obviously—oh, no mistaking it. He's set himself up as some kind of dictator."

"Throwing his weight round," Lee said. "And he was always such a quiet chap. Butter wouldn't melt in his mouth. So now it's a touch of the Hitlers. Or should it be the Mussolinis? And it is to invade Earth?"

Maver nodded.

"The village is packed with men. Hundreds of them. More coming in all the time. And the hills"—Maver gestured vaguely—"Adam told me—boasted—more out there, waiting. He said he would have at least a million men waiting, ready to go through the door when it opens."

I asked, "Is that all he wanted to see you for—to show off?"

"No." Maver looked straight at me. "No. For another reason, Morton. He's had time to work on the men of this village. He's sure of their loyalty. Or is almost sure. But those from the other villages are a different matter. There'll be many waverers, those who refuse to believe that he has been through to our dimension and returned here safely. When the time comes—he made no bones about this—there will be many who will be too frightened to follow into the unknown. And he has to be sure they will follow blindly. He has to prove himself to them, prove his courage by venturing into the dangers of the unknown. That is how he has it planned. He has to make himself into some kind of superman in their eyes. Then they will accept him as their leader. He will be able to dominate them, and they will obey his commands without question. Not a new idea . . ."

"Prove to them?" Lee was puzzled. "How the devil does he intend doing that? You mean, wait till the door opens, go through and then come back again?"

"No, Lee." Maver looked down at the table again. "There would be no time for that sort of thing. The men must be waiting, ready to surge through without any delay at all. No—it's something else he has in mind. He wants to do something no other Toparian has ever done before."

I guessed then what was coming. "The Vorted Nests."

"He knows, of course, that you two have been through the force field and returned safely. But he is keeping that knowledge to himself. The Toparians who saw you enter the field are from another village. The people here know nothing of what happened. Adam has worked out a plan. He believes that there is something in your alien make-up that enables you to pass unharmed through the field. So—"

"Escorts," Lee said. "Just the two of us?"

"The three of us," Maver said. "Adam had me brought to him so that he could deliver an ultimatum. If we will go with him into the Vorted Nest he will see that no harm comes to us afterwards."

"And if we refuse?" I asked.

"Not a pleasant alternative, Morton. Quite simply, we will be taken up in the hills, staked down on an exposed slope and left there to wait for the next storm. He explained that this was their usual method of dealing with their criminal element. It was, he further explained, a most painful way of dying."

"Adam?" Lee breathed incredulously. And then burst out, "He's mad!"

"In a way," his uncle agreed placidly, "yes. The megalomania of a man who has tasted power. Not a new thing—at least on our world. He has organised the Toparians as we have already discovered. He has evolved small-arms drill. He has virtually created an army. He issued his ultimatum from behind a table with a line of armed men at his back. Impressive in its way."

"You agreed, sir," I said, not making a question of it.

"I did. On the principle of while there is life, there is hope. There can be no doubt that our refusal would mean our deaths. He was not bluffing. And if we come safely out of the Vorted Nest we may still have a chance of putting a spoke in his invasion plan."

He added, "I said earlier that I would give a great deal to be able to see inside one of the Nests for myself. Now it seems my wish is to be granted."

It was a sensible decision. The only decision. We would be furthering the plan to invade Earth, but refusing to agree to Adam's demands wouldn't prevent that invasion. I felt certain he would go ahead with that, waverers or no. One thing was for sure: being staked on a hillside at the mercy of the next storm wouldn't help Earth any.

But there was something about Adam wanting to prove himself a superman that didn't ring true. Maybe power had gone to his head, but I couldn't see a man whom Maver had described as intelligent risking his life merely to ensure the blind obedience of his followers. There had to be another reason—a much more important one. And then it came to me, and I jerked my head up to meet Maver's gaze.

"An alliance?" I breathed.

"That is what I think, Morton. Proving himself is only part of it. I know something of the way Adam's mind works, distorted though his reason is at the present time. When he laid his ultimatum in front of me, to balance our deaths he chose to mention only one reason for his going ito the Nest—the reason I would be most likely to accept.

"And the other reason . . . The Toparians have the perfect offensive weapon in the shape of the heat-ray, but they have no defence. The Vorteds have the force field, the perfect defence, but, as far as we know, no offensive weapons. Put the two together . . ." His shrug was expressive.

"An invincible invasion," I said in a voice I didn't recognise.

Lee stared at us. "A conference table. Vorteds and Toparians. God . . ." And then: "Are we still going through with it?"

"It alters nothing," Maver said. "We have no option." He tugged at his nose. "It seems we are less heroic than Adam gave us credit for. Less self-sacrificing. But with more plain common sense."

"When are we supposed to go?" I asked.

"When Adam is ready, he will send for us. Soon."

Lee, over his shock, lifted an eyebrow at me. "Fancy another stroll through the woods, Gerald?"

"Not particularly."

"Afraid of what they might dream up for us this time? Or are you thinking about that private view you had?" Lee turned to his uncle. "We haven't told you about that. That time we went deliberately

through the damned force field Gerald here was
treated to a special display. Nature in the raw with a
vengeance, according to him. I didn't see it."

"See what?" the Professor asked me sharply.

I described briefly the weird landscape of mist,
bubbling pools, and contorted trees.

"But it could have been just another of their tricks,
sir," I added. "Or even a sort of after-effect of going
through the mist. It was only there for a few seconds.
And I was in pretty poor shape at the time. Going
through the field is no joke."

Lee's grin was back.

"And that's an understatement if ever I heard one."
He tugged at his ear. "I wonder if the Vorteds will
decide to show themselves on our next visit?"

They came for us about an hour later, a gang of
grimfaced, armed Toparians, herding us unceremoni-
ously out of the house and marching us towards the
centre of the village. In an open space there, perhaps
a hundred or more of them were assembled, drawn
up in rough ranks of three. Four stood apart from the
rest, deep in discussion. And one of them wore a kind
of fur forage-cap, the first headgear I had seen in this
dimension.

Lee dug his elbow in my ribs. "Friend Adam," said
he.

Clearly, the professor's erstwhile assistant had
dressed to fit the role he had made for himself, using
what materials were at his disposal. His tunic was
more elaborate than those of the rest. A large round
glass ornament hung from a cord about his neck.
Glass decorations on the shoulders had some semblance of badges of rank. A glass emblem adorned
the front of his hat.

I had my first sight of his features when, legs apart,
hands set on hips, shoulders thrown well back, Adam

turned to glare in our direction. Like the faces of his fellow-Toparians, his swarthy one wouldn't have drawn a second glance back on Earth. The hair that curled from beneath his hat was black. His nose was perhaps broader than usual, and there was a wide space between it and his thick-lipped mouth. An ordinary face made arrogant by the expression of the moment.

He swung back to his listeners, apparently to issue orders. One Toparian stepped back smartly enough, raising one hand to his chest in a kind of salute. Children playing soldiers, I thought. But this was no game. Notwithstanding their resemblance to a musical comedy, Adam's simulated uniform and strutting gait, the men drawn up in their ranks, and the outlandish salute were all part of the domination of one man over the rest, the trappings of dictatorship.

After that first glance he completely ignored us. Striding away, he barked orders as he went. A projector jabbing into my back sent me stumbling forward. Lee and his uncle were treated the same. And so the expedition set off for the Vorted Nest—Adam leading the way, a small group of Toparians at his heels, then we three, the centre of an escort of a score of more brown-faced men.

We were not permitted to talk. That was made abundantly clear right at the onset when Lee, refusing to be awed by the pseudo-military appearance of the party, muttered a comment about toy soldiers and received another jab in the ribs for his pains. After that, we marched in silence.

I tried not to think of the coming discomfort of the passage through the mist or of what might be waiting for us on the other side. I had to force myself not to dwell upon what might happen when the door to our own dimension opened again. The sensible thing, I tried to persuade myself, was to make my mind a blank and live from minute to minute.

For a while we marched on level ground, a kind of wide, natural highway leading from the village and skirting the lower slopes of the hills. When this began to narrow, we swung away and started to climb. At the crest of the incline we dropped down into a narrow ravine. Although I felt that Lee and I had probably come this way before, it was all strange to me. I was unable to pick out any familiar landmarks until, emerging from the ravine into a desolation of tumbled rock, I glanced back. I discovered that this was the way we had earlier approached the village, only instead of passing through the ravine we had climbed the slopes to take the long way round.

Some distance ahead, outlined faintly against the eternal haze, there was our hill—a shape that I would never forget. The Toparians in the hollow sprang to their feet at our approach, standing in a line, one of them using the hand-on-chest salute. We passed the other hollow, the one that contained the flimsy-looking wooden platform. Adam swung to the left then, leading the way between tall, needle-pinnacles of rock. At the top of another incline he stopped, waiting for the rest of us to catch up.

In front was the familiar scene of sloping ground, with our hill on the right and the greeny-white curtain of mist on the left, my pyramid and spire silhouetted starkly against it.

Adam issued curt commands in his own tongue. Our escort broke ranks to form in a rough semicircle behind us. The observers, I thought; the boys who are going to watch their leader go into the mist and— they hoped—emerge unscathed again. And then they would pass on the news to the rest. All hail, great chief.

We moved forward then, the four of us, Adam gesturing—he seemed reluctant to speak English—for us to move ahead. And that is how we went into the mist—Lee and I side by side, Maver next, Adam bringing up the rear.

CHAPTER FIFTEEN

This time seemed different to me. There was less discomfort and less resistance from the mist—perhaps because I knew what to expect. I had braced myself for the unpleasant shock of contact. Holding my breath, tensing all my muscles, keeping my hands in front of me and moving quickly, I tried to get the torment of transition over and done with as quickly as possible.

But it was unpleasant enough for all that. The mist clung at first, holding me back, its touch a strange blend of tingling heat and cold. It held me, and then gave way in front like curtains being parted. I sensed the mist closing in behind, so that for a moment or two there was the frightening, lonely feeling of being enclosed in some place remote from everywhere else. There was the stomach-heaving sensation of some kind of force surging through my body. The curtains in front withdrew even more so that I was moving with nightmare slowness through a tunnel of vapour.

Then I caught the first whiff of the sickly-sweet animal smell. Choking, I put my hands to my face, and over my fingers saw the last vestiges of mist dissolve into nothing. I had come through the Vorted force field to emerge, not into a glade of emerald grass, colourful flowers, and statuesque trees, but to stand on the fringe of that frightening, alien landscape I had glimpsed once before.

The ground felt firm enough under my feet. It sloped down gently to what seemed a stream of sluggish, barely-moving grey water. Beyond was the dim nightmare landscape of coiling mist tentacles, bubbling, heaving pools, and grotesque plants and trees.

There was no sunshine. Overhead was a thunderous mass of cloud, hanging so motionless no wind could have moved it, hanging so low it seemed I could have reached up to touch it. The light that filtered down was almost the cold leaden grey of a late November evening on Earth, when hedges and trees are flattened shapes against the cold sky and nothing can be seen distinctly. But here, in this alien place, the leafless plants and contorted, bleached bushes seemed to move in the mist tendrils with some unholy life of their own. What little of the desolate landscape was visible made me inexpressibly thankful that I was not alone. Lee had come to stand on one side of me, the Professor and Adam on the other. It was impossible to tell from their faces in this pale light how they had weathered their passages through the force field, what their reactions were to the scene in front.

Maver was the first to break the silence.

"No apparent sign of animal life," he observed calmly, clinically.

"What in Hades could live in a place like this?" Lee asked in an awe-stricken voice. "Is this what you saw that other time, Gerald?"

"Be my guest," I said as steadily as I could.

"I would say," Maver observed evenly, "that this is the place as it really is. The natural habitat of the Vorteds."

He moved forward to stoop over the sluggish grey stream, inspecting it closely.

It was narrow, barely three feet across, a man's long stride. Whatever the stuff was, it certainly wasn't stagnant water or anything like that. To me, standing now at Maver's side, it seemed more solid than liquid. But for all that, it was in constant movement; not lengthways, as one might have expected, but up and down, pulsating, as if the putty-grey matter was only a crust, a skin beneath which something fought slowly and painfully to escape. And it was from that pink-veined, moving grey substance that the smell was coming. I stepped back hastily, choking a little. Maver, seemingly impervious to its unpleasantness, straightened, frowned, and rubbed his cheek with pensive fingers.

"Is it possible—?" he wondered aloud, and let it go at that, looking about him with narrowed eyes.

Watching him, waiting for him to finish what he had started to say, I became aware of the old sensation of being watched by invisible eyes. The sensation may have been there from the first moment of our entering the Vorted Nest, but it was only now I noticed it.

The Professor seemed content to stand there, looking about him with interested eyes. I felt some easing of my fears in his calm assessment of our surroundings. Adam made the first move. Without speaking he went to the brink of the stream, hesitated a moment, and then stepped across. On the far side, his feet set on what seemed solid black soil, he suddenly swayed, arms outflung as he fought to keep his balance. Lee went over next, then Maver and I together. Under my

feet I could feel the ground give, as if I were standing on a thin coating of soil beneath which lava bub-
bled and writhed.

But thankfully, only a pace or two away, was the
start of a path—a path made of solid-seeming pieces
of stone. Strangely, I couldn't recall having noticed
that path when we had stood on the far bank, but
there it was now, meandering away between bubbling, geyser-like pools and clumps of slimy, bleached
plants to become lost in the grey murk.

Adam, still taking the initiative, stepped onto it.
That it was as solid as it had appeared was patent
from the way he stood upright, no longer swaying,
arms back at his sides. Without waiting, without any
hesitation, he turned to walk along the path. We followed in silence. It was a great relief to feel firm
ground beneath my feet again.

Although the causeway was more than wide enough
to take two abreast, Adam still walked on alone. Always a few paces ahead, he never once turned to be
reassured that we were behind. Although I had come
to regard him as an enemy, I found myself admiring
him for his courage, for the way he stalked with head
up and shoulders back into the greyness of this strange
world of the Vorteds, which certainly he must have
been taught from childhood to fear.

On either hand was the unstable black soil, its
moist surface broken by round pools of oily, black-
looking liquid. Bubbles rose slowly to the surface,
bursting, releasing small clouds of yellow mist. Apart
from the pad of our feet the only sound to break the
oppressive stillness was the almost continual soft plop-
ping of the bursting bubbles.

We walked without knowing where we were going,
where the path would take us to. It was far more hot
in here than even in the midday sun outside. Sweat
streamed down our faces, soaked our clothes. The

evil smell seemed to be getting stronger. Lee remarked on it in a low voice, adding—looking un-
easily about him—that he had the old feeling of being watched. I looked back over my shoulder, finding
that the mist had closed in behind. There was no sign
of the thicker, different-coloured force field. Behind
was the same spine-chilling desolation as in front.

The path changed direction to pass between low
jagged peaks of black rock. The smooth surfaces glistened with an oily sheen. Scabrous-topped fungi,
bloated shapes with long stems and hanging gills, protruded from crannies.

Emerging from the ravine the path passed between
long chains of pools, all circular, all filled with that
slow-bubbling tar-like liquid, almost touching each
other, only separated by clumps of pallid, elongated
leafless plants.

With no means of telling the passage of time, with
little change in the scenery to break the evil monot-
ony, we seemed to have been walking for hours. Despite the many changes of direction, I felt sure we
were heading towards the centre of the Nest. And I
felt equally sure—knowing of some of the Vorteds'
capabilities—that the path had been put there for
just that purpose.

After a while another grey stream, almost a duplicate of the first one we had encountered, came to run
at one side of the causeway, following its bends and
curves. If we had wanted to, we could not have
crossed this one; it was far too wide.

The stream left us at a place where the path swung
to follow the flanks of another and much larger outcropping of slime-coated black rock. High at one
side, the rock sloped down to a level-topped plateau,
at its lowest point little more than a couple of feet
above the surface of the ground. It looked like a
black island in a black sea, almost like a ship.

When we rounded the island we found a change in the scene ahead. Adam stopped. Maver went to stand on one side of him, Lee and I on the other.

I was first struck by the odd way in which the mist some distance ahead seemed to have withdrawn, collecting itself, forming a dense white curtain to enclose the scene. To one side was a cluster of what seemed to be ordinary green-foliaged trees. In front of them —in this uncanny halflight they seemed to float a few inches above the ground—was a collection of about a dozen houses, built of pale stone, circular in shape, with domed, beehive tops. It was impossible to believe that anything could live in this terrible place. But people, or beings, did live here, for these were their houses and there, standing a little to one side, were the beings themselves.

The distance, the dim light, and the drifting tendrils of grey mist made it impossible to see them clearly. Like their homes, they seemed to be suspended above the ground. They were the size and shape of men, and they seemed to be watching us, for I had the impression of faces turned in our direction. I think there were seven of them, but even that was hard to tell. We would have to go much, much closer before we could hope to get any idea of what they really looked like. And I, for one, felt very reluctant to take even one step nearer.

There was no hesitation on Adam's part. I felt I could read his thoughts—as undoubtedly the Vorteds had already done—and so know what was in his mind. He had collected his courage to make the journey to this frightening place for the main purpose of proposing an alliance with its inhabitants. He had come so far, and there they were, waiting for him.

He strode unhesitatingly towards them, throwing off Maver's restraining hand, ignoring his cry of warning. He walked along the path that led straight to the collection of strange houses. His shape dwindled as he narrowed the distance between himself and the waiting Vorteds.

And I knew, I could feel, that something was very wrong.

Adam had almost reached them when the transformation came. The trees, the houses, and the weird white shapes suddenly collapsed, dissolving, melting into the ground. The curtain of mist was swept away, revealing a vast, smooth-topped brown mound of what was most certainly the same rubbery pulsating substance of which the streams were composed. And from the base of that awesome mound a brown sea lapped out, reaching towards Adam's feet, engulfing them. We saw him struggle to free himself. And then we heard him scream.

CHAPTER SIXTEEN

I had never before heard a man scream in agony. I think I found the sound more shocking than the sight of his struggle. For an instant we were all stunned into immobility. That the trapped man was an enemy made no difference. He was a human being—a man like any other in appearance—and he was in the grip of something horrifyingly alien and unnatural. The smell was indescribably evil, almost overpowering. And, even worse, a hideous hissing, churning sound came from that mass of pulsating, heaving matter.

The shock passed and I leaped forward automatically, aware of movements at my side that were Lee and his uncle doing the same. The matter lapped about Adam's feet and seemed to be climbing his ankles. He screamed again, terribly, struggling desperately to free himself. Fighting revulsion and fear, I stood on the fringe of that brown tide, reaching out my hand. He grasped it with the fury of a drowning man clutching a straw. For a terrifying moment I swayed, almost losing my balance, almost being pulled forward to go sprawling face down into the stuff. Then Lee's arm came to clamp round my waist, steadying me, then pulling me back. One of Adam's feet came free with a glutinous sucking sound. Despite Lee's help I fell to my knees, Adam's hand still grasping mine, the two only inches above that throbbing surface. And then, unexpectedly, miraculously, the living tide parted, drawing back, leaving Adam's other foot free. The sudden relief of tension sent me rolling over backwards, Adam flying after me head first.

Lee dragged him away while I was pulling myself together and regaining my feet. Adam had lost consciousness. I helped Lee by taking hold of Adam's feet. Urged on by the Professor, guided by him, we carried the unconscious man away from the mound, stumbling on ground that had suddenly become unstable, that gave beneath our feet. We carried our burden to the flat-topped island of rock, dragged him up onto the top and there laid him down. Panting, I looked back to find that the mist had dropped again, hiding the monstrous mound from view. But I could still hear the churning sound; its stench still filled my nostrils.

Maver was stooping over Adam's feet. The sandals had gone completely, and the fur gaiters hung in shreds. The exposed flesh was seared and brilliant scarlet, the skin broken in parts, blood seeping and trickling.

Maver touched that inflamed, partly decomposed flesh and then straightened slowly, turning to look in the direction of the now shrouded mound. He nodded almost with satisfaction, as if confirming some private theory.

Taking off his shirt, Lee knelt at the unconscious man's side, ripping the cloth, making rough bandages to bind about the mutilated feet. I went to help. He looked up wonderingly at his uncle.

"Acid," he said. "That's what it looks like. For all the world as if acid had been spilled over his feet."

And the Professor nodded. "Yes, Lee. That is what it is. Hydrochloric acid. Or its equivalent. But much more potent. Digestive fluid."

Lee paused in his bandaging to wonder anew. "Digestive fluid?"

"You are going to find this hard to believe." The other pointed at Adam's feet. "That is what happens to food in your stomach. Or rather, the start of the process. The process of digestion. How can I explain it to you? I have had the idea at the back of my mind ever since we entered this place. What I have seen since confirms my belief. Now I am sure. The dwellings we saw, the beings, even the path we came by, were not real, not part of the true things of this place."

That was obvious. "Like our glades and woods," I said.

"Like those, Morton. But they were not hallucinations. They were composed of solid matter, the matter of this place which had become temporarily modified so that it assumed other shapes and forms. As a chameleon changes its colour to blend with its surroundings.

"Adam had his own mental picture of what he thought a Vorted village and its occupants might look like. This place simply took the picture from his mind and used its substance to create such a village as the final bait in the trap."

I think I had a glimmering then of what he was going to tell us.

"What is this place?" I asked.

"It is difficult to find words for something that is so alien to our way of thinking. We cannot rightly call it a 'place.' A being? No." He shook his head. "Something for which we do have a word, but that word is inadequate for what it has to describe here. All this, everything you see about you, everything that is enclosed within the force field which is not, after all, a force field at all, is one thing—a Vorted, for want of a better term. One Vorted."

He paused while he collected words, moving to stand on the edge of our island.

"Long ago, when the whirling, suspended particles of matter became changed, coming together again, finally to settle, instead of forming many creatures as I had first suspected, they formed only the one, small at first, now grown to this gigantic size. And still growing. It is a thing that is part mineral, part plant, part animal. And it is one single gigantic cell.

"Its composition is a duplicate of a simple plant cell as seen under the microscope. The mist which encloses it—overhead as well as about its circumference —is the outer covering, the skin, the equivalent of the cellulose walls of a plant cell. This unstable black substance which has all the appearance of soil is the cytoplasm, made up of waste matter and stored food— metaplasm. The pools are the spaces in the cytoplasm —the vacuoles. And that, of course—" He pointed in the direction of the invisible mound.

"The nucleus," I said tonelessly.

"One may indeed regard it as such," he agreed. "But because of the animal element, a much more complex affair. It will contain the brain, the heart, the nerve centre. It is also the stomach, for it is obvious from what we just witnessed that food is trapped there, absorbed and digested, and then certainly transmitted to all parts of the cell by means of the streams. And they are simply extensions of the stomach."

Lee had finished his bandaging and was crouching back on his heels, over the shock of the Professor's pronouncement, staring about him with mingled amazement and disbelief.

"All this is just the one thing?" And: "Five miles or more across?" And something that was even more incredible, and frightening: "We're actually inside it?"

Maver smiled faintly at his tone.

"I can well understand your disbelief. But that is the way of it, Lee. We could be compared with virus in a bloodstream. Or, more appropriately"—his voice was dryness itself—"with food that has been swallowed but has yet to reach the digestive organs."

Lee scrambled to his feet.

"For God's sake!" he cried. "Let's get the hell out of here!"

"My sentiments entirely," Maver said, still in that dry tone. "Nothing would give me greater pleasure. I have seen all I want to see. But"—going to stand at Adam's side—"we have a responsibility. We know what the ground will be like to walk on. It would be impossible to carry him for any distance. We will have to wait until he regains consciousness. Let us hope he will be able to walk. In the meantime we seem reasonably secure on this rock. How long that security will last I have no idea. One has the impression that our friend is mulling over the problem of what to do with us."

I looked about me. The drifting grey mist seemed to have thickened. There was no sign now of the path by which we had come. But I had expected that. The Vorted had made it to bring us here; it would certainly not let it remain as a means of return.

But something was puzzling me—had been nagging at my thoughts for some time. The mound, the nucleus, had actually trapped a victim, and then let him go again. We hadn't pulled Adam free; the brown matter had withdrawn of its own accord. And that didn't make sense.

I couldn't think of any explanation, but I didn't feel like putting the problem to the Professor. Not right now, not while we had the more important problem—of how to get out of this . . . this thing—to solve.

Five miles in diameter, and we were at the very heart. Well over two miles to travel, on ground that would give at every step, with an injured man on our hands—assuming he did regain consciousness—and at the end, with no way of telling if the mist would allow us to pass through.

Hands on hips, Lee looked down at Adam's bandaged feet.

"The best I could do," he said. "At least the soles weren't too badly"—he faltered over the word—"digested. The thick sandals must have protected them. All the same, he won't be in fit state to do much walking." He gazed around. "Nothing we can use to make a litter." He stamped on the rock. "Solid enough, thank God. Like Gibraltar. But why? I mean, why doesn't this blasted Vorted try dislodging us?"

The Professor rubbed his jaw.

"That is only one of the things I find confusing, Lee. Our rock is part of the mineral content or the cell. As such, one would think the Vorted would cause it to change, so that it would no longer protect us. For some reason the cell seems wary of us, making no further attempt to entice or force us to its stomach."

I went to stand by Adam, looking down at him. The sulphurous light glinted dully on the tawdry glass on breast and shoulders. His hat—I felt it must be precious to him—had been lost in his struggle with the brown tide. At that moment I felt sorry for this pathetic little man who had set himself up as a petty dictator. God knows, no matter how evil his intent, he didn't deserve to suffer in this way. When all was said and done, we were really to blame; it was during his stay in our world that he had learned about such things. But that didn't alter the matter. He was still our enemy.

Beyond him, a cluster of white-stemmed leafless plants grew above the rim of our plateau. Looking at them—wondering absently if they were poisonous —I remembered the way the branch had behaved in the glade. On an impulse I picked up a strip of cloth left over from Lee's ministrations and wrapped it about my hands. Thus protected to some extent I reached out to grasp one of the stems. As my fingers neared it, so it swayed back out of reach. I tried again, with the same result. A movement at my side was Lee, his face curious. In silence I unwound the cloth and handed it to him. In silence he wrapped it about his hand and then reached out as I had done. And the plant stayed still, letting him grasp it. He snapped off two of the stems and let them fall along with the cloth to the rock.

"Like before," he said. "Damn it, Gerald, there's got to be some reason—"

And then Adam stirred and opened his eyes.

I kicked the stems over the edge of the plateau. Like before. Yes. And other things: the way that brown sea had moved away from my hand. But only when my hand had come close to it. There had to be something about me that was different. For some reason I had repelled a branch, the brown tide, now the plants. I lifted my hand, staring at it, puzzling over its ordinary appearance.

And then, you know, realisation came. It was incredible, simple, but it was logical. It made sense. But before I finally accepted the explanation there was one final experiment I must make. That would have to wait.

Adam, helped by Lee and Maver, had managed to get to his feet. I went to lend my assistance. The Toparian, eyes glazed, looked down at his feet. He shuddered as memory returned, looking in the direction of the mist-shrouded mound. The hissing, churning sound was more than enough to make memory hideously complete. He shuddered again, violently, taking a stumbling step backwards.

Maver took hold of his shoulder, steadying him, asking: "How do you feel?" And: "Do you think you will be able to walk?"

The other shook himself free of the steadying hand with an impatient, almost angry movement, and tried a few steps.

"I can walk," he said through tight lips, and that was all—no gratitude offered, no word, no look even for Lee and me. And no questions addressed to the Professor.

"At least the going will be soft enough," Lee said wryly. "Too soft, I'm thinking. You'll have noticed our path has done a vanishing act. Looks like we've a long cake-walk in front of us. I remember going on one of those in a fun fair when I was a kid. The same sort of feeling . . ."

"We must avoid the pools," Maver said. "They are an unknown quantity. So are the various specimens of growing things. And, of course, the nuclear extensions . . . The stream-like—ah—affairs," he added for Adam's benefit. "Undoubtedly, they will be the greatest hazard. We will have to resist any attempt on the part of the ground to force us in their direction."

"All set for a pleasant little stroll then," Lee said, and sat on the edge of the plateau. He let his feet down carefully and stood upright on the black soil, swaying, observing that it was "like trying to walk on treacle," and then crying out in startled pain as thin, pallid tendrils lashed out from some hidden crevice to wrap themselves tightly about his arm.

I went to his aid and, as I had hoped, my touch was enough to make them relax and sway writhing away.

"The magic touch," he gasped, rubbing his arm. "I knew it would come in useful sooner or later. Thanks, Gerald. You'd better stay handy . . ."

The incident, happening so quickly, seemed to have escaped the Professor's notice. But then he was taken up with helping Adam limp painfully across the plateau. When they reached the rim I steadied the Toparian while he lowered himself to the soil. Maver stepped down next and I followed. The ground gave under my feet as I had expected. It was, as Lee had described it, like treading on a thick layer of treacle.

And so we set off on the return journey. For reasons of my own I put myself in the lead, leaving Lee and his uncle to follow, supporting Adam between them. The only thing to help me select a starting direction was the fact that the nucleus-mound, the plateau, and our original point of entry into this damned thing must be all more or less on a straight line. But once the black island was out of sight, and that would be very soon, I would have nothing left save my sense of direction.

It didn't let me down. As we made our slow, swaying step-by-lurching-step progress I was able to recall certain landmarks from our inward journey: the chains of pools and the ravine between the slime-covered rock pinnacles. And, again for reasons of my own, I kept my pace slower than it need have been, allowing no space to come between myself and those following. That Lee trod on my heels several times and was inclined to mutter annoyed impatience at my snail-like progress made no difference.

We stopped from time to time to allow Lee and Maver to change places. I felt guilty at not offering to take one of their places and do my bit in helping Adam, who, despite his earlier assurance, was incapable of walking unaided. But I couldn't do that because I wanted my arms free. I hoped with all my heart that the conclusion I had privately reached was the right one. If it wasn't, I felt certain we would not be allowed to leave this place. I would know for certain, I told myself, when we arrived at the mist-covering of the Vorted.

Oddly, for all our very slow progress, the return journey seemed to take less time than had the inward one. But that was only my own assessment, almost certainly rising from the fact I had so much on my mind. I had to concentrate all the time upon what I was doing. From moment to moment I had to hold myself ready for any move on the part of the Vorted to force us from our path. But no such attempt was made. I could only think that the intelligence was relying upon its covering of mist to prevent our final escape. I had to concentrate upon trying to pierce the drifting tenacles ahead, choosing a route that gave the greatest margin of safety between the bubbling pools. Detours were necessary to avoid clumps of growing things, and making those detours I had to keep our original direction always in mind.

One moment I was leading a cautious way between a mass of thread-thin, wax-white tendrils and an outcropping of knife-edged black rock. The next I was coming out onto open ground with the stream of the nuclear extension almost at my feet, and behind, the motionless green-tinged curtain of mist.

Relief that we had come this far was replaced by apprehension that the time had come for my experiment, and that our lives depended upon its outcome. I stepped over the stream and then turned to help in the hazardous business of lifting Adam over. We managed it with some effort, lowering him to the strangely solid ground, where he leaned back on his hands, head back, eyes closed, his chest rising and falling painfully. He was in a sorry state: sweat streaming down a face drawn with pain, his fur tunic open to the waist, blood showing through the bandages on his feet. For a few minutes we rested in that no-man's-land between the living stream and the living skin of the cell.

When Maver made the first move I slipped quickly past him, with the dual purposes of helping Lee tug Adam back to his feet and letting the Professor now take the lead and so be the first one to enter the mist barrier.

He plunged into it and was immediately brought to a halt, still visible to us, held there while he struggled without result, almost seeming to be suspended above the ground, his arms spread wide. He struggled —we could see how he fought to move forward— then, realising the futility, he fell back, staggering, turning a face filled with dismay in our direction.

"No—" he gasped. "It's no use . . ."

The first part of my experiment was over. It had been successful. And now . . .

"Maybe if we all try together," I suggested. "A wedge—with me in the lead, the same way we came in."

He shook his head. "It's useless, Morton . . ." But stunned, he still came to take my place at Adam's side. "You saw what happened. It has changed . . . I think I anticipated this. But I hoped . . . Now it is impenetrable."

Lee said doubtfully, "It doesn't look any different."

"It is living matter, able to change its consistency without altering in appearance. Its original purpose would most certainly have been to protect the vulnerable parts of the cell against damage by the magnetic storms. It is also strong enough to resist the Toparian heat-rays. Matter that is so strong will certainly be able to resist our passage through it if the Vorted is so inclined. For obvious reasons it allowed us to enter. It will not let us escape."

"We can but try," I said.

His shrug was a mixture of annoyance and impatience. "If you must satisfy yourself . . ."

So we formed a wedge with myself as the apex. I knew that it wasn't because we all entered the mist at the same time that it parted to allow us through. It was because I was in the lead. I thrust forward, giving myself no time to think. The mist resisted and then gave, forming a tunnel. There was the now familiar sensation of force flooding through my body and then I was out, out into the dazzling sunlight with the others only a pace behind. Relief was so intense as to bring a feeling of sickness.

At first the light was too fierce for eyes accustomed to the grey dimness of the cell. Shielding them, I blinked tears away. Gradually my vision cleared. We had emerged from the Vorted only a short distance from our original point of entry. There—I could see it now through narrowed eyes—over to the left was our hill. But not our hill as I had last seen it.

The crude platform Lee and I had examined in the hollow had been set in position, almost at the top of the slope. My gaze lifted automatically. I think I knew what I was to see there, hanging in the sky, even before I was able to focus on that flickering, wavering oblong of light. Relief flooded again, and unimaginable joy. They were emotions that died as my eyes moved back down to the hill.

There they were, the Toparians; countless numbers of them it seemed, gathered in a silent watching crowd, a multitude, all armed with the heat-projectors. They crowded our hill, they were massed on adjoining slopes, they were packed in every hollow and ravine. They were everywhere—except for one place. There was a reason why they had left empty the stretch of level ground at the foot of the hill. That was the ground that lay in front of the mist.

And the mist—the skin of the cell—was moving. Slowly, creeping forward so slowly, inching its way towards the hill and the door.

The platform had been set immediately beneath the lambent oblong in the sky, so that a man had but to mount the ladder, take three steps and he would be on the threshold of the door. And all they were waiting for, this multitude of fur-tunicked men, was their leader. They would be ready now to follow him through into our world.

The Vorted must have known that too. Which was why it was moving, why the mist was changing its shape, sending out a feeler towards the foot of the hill.

CHAPTER SEVENTEEN

An age ago—it seemed an age—Lee, only half seriously, had envisaged the situation that might arise; three groups of people waiting on the starting line to see which would be the first to reach the door. At the time I had tried to picture the scene. Now, reality was infinitely worse than had been my imagined picture. Worse because it was obvious we three humans stood no chance at all of getting through those massed ranks of Toparians. Even worse still because one of the groups wasn't a group at all, but one monstrous thing. And it was that thing, that single, gigantic, intelligent cell, that was making the first move towards the door. Creeping slowly forward, with the Toparians falling back in front, keeping their distance, not even bothering to use against it weapons they knew to be futile.

Standing helplessly there, I had a vivid mental image of the Vorted reaching the door and flowing through it. Through into the laboratory where Leming would be waiting. It would wrap itself about him and move relentlessly on, out into the farmyard, spreading slowly into the fields, absorbing the richness of earth as it went, finding the food that had been lacking in its own dimension, able to grow more and more quickly, spreading, engulfing, covering everywhere. . . .

I had to fight to cleanse my thoughts of that terrifying picture. There was perhaps one chance of thwarting the Toparians' intentions. Not a good chance, and to take it I would have to act quickly. I had to talk to Adam; I had to try to make a bargain with him. And to do that, I would have to take advantage of his dazed condition, using the truth and a great deal of bluff.

He stood alone, refusing assistance now that he was in the presence of his people, unsteady on his feet, but with his head up, shoulders proudly back. Although he must be aware of the urgency, Adam seemed too proud to make a move to rally his followers until he had regained sufficient strength to walk unaided.

Lee and his uncle had moved a short distance away, standing there, watching the scene on the hill, their faces filled with consternation. It was now or never. I went to stand at Adam's side. He ignored my presence until I spoke.

"We know why you wanted to go through the mists," I said, and at that he turned cold eyes on me. "You were hoping to form an alliance with the Vorteds."

And I hoped to God that I wouldn't have to waste precious time in telling what the Vorted Nest really was. On our way back from the nucleus I had heard them talking behind me. I hoped fervently that Maver had been explaining everything to him.

"You saw what it is like in there," I said. "There are no such people as Vorteds. All that—"

He knew, and broke in curtly: "Save your breath."

Over the first hurdle. "We helped you in there," I said. "We saved your life. Now it lies within your power to help us."

I was conscious of sounding over-dramatic, my phraseology pompous and flowery. But that, I felt, would be the most likely way of making an impression on him.

"I was expecting that." His features were impassive. "No. The future of my people is far more important than the repayment of a trivial personal debt."

I had expected something along those lines, a self-satisfied reply that could have been lifted from any third-rate melodrama. I wondered how much of his spare time in our world had been spent at the cinema.

Now I had to press on with this unreal interchange in an attempt to smash through his façade of complacent superiority. I swung to point towards the hill.

"You can see what is happening. The Vorted knows where the door leads and is already moving towards it."

"It moves only slowly." He was unshaken, unperturbed. "There is time enough. I am going to my people now. They will follow me when I give the command. We will be first through the door."

When he would have moved I put my hand on his shoulder. He shook it off angrily.

"Some of you will get through," I said as quickly as I could. "But not many. Then, unless you want the Vorted to follow, you will have to close it from the other side. The few of you that have managed to get through will be insufficient for your purpose."

As I half-expected, he had an answer to that.

"We will let the Vorted through. There will be only the one. The others are too far away. One Vorted can do no harm."

"Don't you realise what will happen to it once it reaches our world? Here, in your dimension, its growth has only been slow because of lack of food. Our world is different. You know that. Food is unlimited. It will grow quickly, and you will have no way of stopping it. And it has intelligence. Once it has covered the land it will find a way of crossing the sea. You will be worse off in our world than you have been here."

The first stirring of doubt moved his swarthy features.

"I will make a bargain with you," I said. "I will help you if you will help us."

"A bargain?" His cold smile verged on a sneer. "What have you to bargain with?"

"Knowledge. We were only able to enter the Vorted Nest because I was with you. I was the only one able to save you from the nucleus. We were only able to leave again because I led the way."

"You are talking foolishness," he said roughly, but he was remembering and wavering.

"I know how the Vorteds can be destroyed," I said. "I will trade that knowledge in return for your help in getting us back to our own world."

And when he hesitated, the smug superiority gone at last from his features, conflicting emotions in its place, I rammed the thing home, speaking with all the intensity I could muster.

"I can tell you how to penetrate the mists unharmed. You can use heat-projectors to burn the hearts away. The Vorteds will die. Where they have been will be rich soil on which you can grow food."

I set the alternative in front of him.

"If you refuse the bargain then both your people and mine will be doomed. If you accept, the lot of your people will be infinitely better than it is now. It is as simple as that."

Common sense, on the face of it. Just so long as he

wasn't allowed too much time to think. This was the crisis . . .

And it worked, thank God. My bluff—for that was mainly what it was—worked. But then he was still partly dazed from his experience in the Vorted. And it was obvious he had to make a decision without delay.

"If you have this knowledge," he said curtly, "we trade. Now."

"No." I pointed now to the hill where the creeping mist had reached our cairn of stones. "We trade when we are standing on that platform on the threshold of the door."

He didn't like that. His eyes narrowed with suspicion.

"How do I know you will keep your part of the bargain?"

"You will have to trust me," I told him, and then brought out a pre-prepared offering. "I saved your life when you were an enemy, a threat to my world. I could easily have let you die. But I saw you as a human being. The Vorted is alien to both of us. It would give me great pleasure to see it—all of them— destroyed. Or know that they were going to be destroyed."

And a finishing touch, something I knew could not fail to find its mark: "You will be the only one of your people to know the secret. You will be their saviour. You will mean more to them than you do now."

He stared at me for a long moment and then turned to limp away, shouting commands in his own language. The ranks broke, the dark-faced Toparians moving back, leaving the way clear. Lee and the Professor turned startled looks in my direction. But there was no time for even the briefest of explanations. The Vorted had swallowed the cairn and was moving, more quickly now, up the higher slope.

"Hurry!" I hurled at them, and left the urgency of my voice to do the rest. They moved after me as I followed Adam to the level ground at the base of the hill.

We were only able to go slowly, held back by Adam's limping pace. A quick assessment of the distance between the mist and the platform sent an icy, shuddering wave of apprehension through me. I knew that if we were able to reach the platform only moments ahead of the Vorted, I would be able to hold it back while we went through the door. But I had the feeling from the glowering, openly suspicious Toparian faces turned in our direction that if I were to race ahead they might use their weapons against me. I was only safe so long as I was with their leader.

If the mist reached the door first, we would be too late. Once it started to flow through, there would be nothing I could do to halt its progress. We would have to wait, and that was something I didn't want. It would give Adam time to think. And it wouldn't take him long to realise there were other ways he could take the secret from me without having to bargain for it.

We were climbing the hill now, moving parallel to the creeping mist. The Toparians were on our right and behind us. I glanced quickly at Adam's face. It was frowning, filled with doubt, its message plain. At any moment he was going to come to a halt and call our bargain off. That was when I took the risk of racing ahead. And my guess was right, for he put out his hand to stop me, his grip sliding off my elbow as I went.

I reached the ladder leading up the platform in the same moment that the mist touched it. Momentarily forgetful I grasped one of the uprights with my left hand, using the other to try to ward off the Vorted. Terrifyingly, it ignored me, thickening, wrapping itself about my legs.

Then reason returned. Changing my grip I held out my left hand, and the mist recoiled, drawing back on itself, leaving my legs free again. Lee was panting at my side. I motioned for him to climb, but he waited for Maver to go first. And then Adam was there too, shouting something in his own language, his intention still clear enough although the words meant nothing to me. I pushed him frantically away, more roughly than I had intended, for he went staggering back down the slope.

I knew what the consequences of that would be. Lee had reached the platform on his uncle's heels and I was halfway up the rickety ladder, looking back over my shoulder, when the first heat-ray came lancing slowly towards us, gathering momentum and brilliance as it came. It struck the base of the construction as I scrambled onto the platform. Flames crackled, smoke rose in dark billows, and the platform swayed sickeningly.

The Professor was on his knees—I hadn't seen him stumble—almost on the threshold of the flickering oblong of light. Lee stood over him, trying to pull him back to his feet. Mist surged over the smoke-free side of the platform, a tentacle probing towards me. It coiled sharply back as I warded it off with my hand. A second heat-ray came sweeping towards us. But Maver was on his feet at last and plunging into the blue light of the door, flicking out of existence. Lee turned an anguished face towards me, shouting, the words lost in the roar and crackle of the flames, then swinging round to vanish in his turn through the door.

Now it was my turn. The door was waiting, but there was something I had to do first. I still intended fulfilling my part of the bargain. Adam stood there, one hand to his side, looking up at me through the smoke. I unstrapped my wrist-watch and tossed it down to him. Then, only waiting long enough to see him catch it, I turned to go through the door.

There was the old feeling of plunging down a bottomless lift-shaft, terrifying moments of nothingness, the sickness of forces at work in my body, and then I was sprawling on my hands and knees on the blessed concrete floor of the laboratory. I slipped sideways, catching my head against one corner of the block on which the generators were mounted so that for a few moments I was partly stunned, only vaguely aware of what was going on around me.

Mr. Leming was there, in his shirt sleeves, standing with his back to the bench. And Maver, leaning against the wall, was shouting, "Switch off! For God's sake, Martin, switch off!"

I had an impression of Leming turning to the bench. That picture came as I bounced back from the impact, rolling over on my side with my face close to Lee's feet. Between his legs I could see the dancing blue screen of the magnetic field. And I could see mist seeping through. Then the light flicked out of existence, leaving a thin column of mist hanging in the still, dry air.

Watching it—fearfully watching that small part of a Vorted that had followed us back into our world —I heard Leming say, "You've brought a sample of weather back with you. We've got enough fog of our own . . ." And then: "It's good to see you again, John."

Lee helped me concernedly to my feet. "I'm all right," I told him. "Just a bump on the head."

The mist column was settling slowly. Now it was a coiling white pool hovering on the concrete. Now it was gone.

"Not fog," the Professor said to Leming, eyeing the empty floor. "Something very different. Very different indeed. And how have you been keeping, Martin?"

It was a trite, unemotional greeting that was, in its way, an echo of Lee's not-so-long-ago "Dr. Livingstone, I presume?"

"You have all the appearance of having had a rough time," Leming observed mildly. He turned his gaze on Lee and me. "You two, also. Sadly the worse for wear." He eyed us carefully from head to toe. "How you have been able to get in such a state in such a short space of time is past belief."

Lee asked: "What day is it, sir? What is the time?"

"What day?" Leming's brows lifted almost comically.

"We have experienced some discrepancy in the passage of time," Maver explained vaguely.

"I see. Interesting. I look forward to hearing all about it. In the meantime you wish to get your bearings, as it were. It is still Saturday morning." Leming elaborately consulted his watch. "The time is a few minutes after eight-fifteen. If you, Morton and Miller, require more details, your absence was noticed by Mrs. Robson at seven-fifteen when she came over to the laboratory after having failed to contact you by phone. She broke the news to me some five minutes later. I spared time only to dress myself. Then I started work immediately. That would be approximately three-quarters of an hour ago. I happened upon the necessary combination of readings only seconds before your somewhat violent return. Does that satisfy you? It seems you are all in urgent need of the services of a bathroom. You may also be hungry. Mrs. Robson has, of course, delayed breakfast." Breakfast . . . I met Lee's eye.

"Something," said he, "more palatable than water and mush."

We had taken turns to make use of the bathroom. We had changed into clean clothes, and breakfast was over. In the sun-filled lounge Professor Maver told his story to Leming. I left it to Lee to supply our quota.

It was an abridged version, at least so far as Maver was concerned; I had the feeling that he and Leming would later go through the whole thing again, in greater detail, probably making notes as they went along. But there it was. Maver told his part, Lee added his bit, and Maver rounded the whole thing off from the point where our ways had met and linked. It wasn't until the end that I was allowed my little say, such as it was.

"There are certain—ah—facets," Maver said blandly, "which require elucidation. Perhaps Morton here can add a little more to the story. I notice that he is no longer wearing his wrist-watch. I ask myself —has he discarded it simply because he had come to realise its uselessness?"

So he knew. I was disappointed.

"I didn't bring it back with me," I said, wondering when he had realised its significance.

"You gave it to Adam?"

"Yes," I said, and Lee asked petulantly: "What's so damned unusual about Gerald's watch?"

"Let it be Morton's privilege to tell us," Maver said smugly. And then went on to cancel out some of that privilege before I even had chance to open my mouth.

"He was the one, you recall, who led us through the mist. It was his intervention that prevented Adam being digested. It was from his hands—his hand, rather—that the living matter of the Vorted recoiled.

And you will also recall that when I attempted on my own to force through the mist I was unable to do so. But it parted to allow Morton, and so the rest of us, to pass through. It seemed obvious that he was in possession of something abhorrent, even dangerous, to the matter of the cell. Process of elimination led to his watch."

"It had a luminous dial," I said.

"And so was radioactive," Maver supplied. "Only to a very small degree, of course, not enough to do the slightest harm to a human being. But still enough to set a Geiger counter ticking. And more than enough to make itself felt in a place where there is no such thing as radioactivity.

"Perhaps"—he nodded to himself—"it was present in the dimension at one time, but was nullified in some way by the magnetic devices used during the war. Certainly, as we know from Adam's stay here, a small amount of radioactivity has no adverse effects upon the Toparians. But a living organism such as the cell, born after the war, was affected by it."

He turned back to me. "And you told Adam?"

"I gave him the watch and left him to figure it out for himself," I said, and then went on to explain about the bargain I had made.

"It was partly bluff," I said at the end. "I had to rely upon Adam's dazed condition and the fact he had other things on his mind. It was a question of stampeding him into accepting before he had time to think it all out. I mean, he could have used force to make me disgorge the secret. And once he knew about the watch, we wouldn't have stood a chance. Apart from anything else, he would have known that if the Vorted had managed to get into our world, our radioactivity would have killed it eventually. The fall-out from nuclear tests . . ."

"When did you find out about the watch?" Lee demanded resentfully.

"When we were in the cell," I said. "But I wasn't sure at first. It was only because I wear it on my left wrist and I happen to be left-handed that I found out. I didn't know for sure until we came back through the mist."

But Leming, it seemed, was more interested in the Vorted than in the means of its destruction.

"Your surmise, John," said he, leaning forward intently, "is that it was the product of . . ."

We left them to it, Lee and I. We went out into the sunshine where trees and flowers were real trees and flowers. Birds were whistling as birds ought to whistle, and white flecks of happy-looking cloud drifted across a pale blue sky.

We left the laboratory alone . . .

"I've seen enough of that place to last me a lifetime," Lee said feelingly as we walked by the metal door. "I wonder if Uncle John intends to dismantle his equipment?"

"I hope so," I said fervently.

In the knee-high grass behind the concrete building, Lee counted steps. "Fifteen, sixteen . . ." He stopped to look back, assessing the distance. "Just about here was where we built the cairn."

We wandered on. The trees thinned. A smooth green bank sloped to a gently-trickling stream.

"And here," Lee said. "Smack inside the Vorted."

"Quite a thought," I said, when something seemed expected of me.

"A watch . . ." He couldn't get over it. "A stupid, paltry, tin-pot watch . . ."

"It was a good one," I said with some regret. "It was the first one I'd ever owned. I can remember buying it. I chose one in the window and then I went into the shop. The man behind the counter had a way with him. I didn't particularly need a watch with a luminous dial. He talked me into it."

"I wonder what he'd say," he mused, "if he knew where it had finished up?"

We turned to make our way back to the house.

THE
ANDROMEDA
STRAIN

by Michael Crichton

This is the breathtaking story of "Project Wildfire"—the crash mobilization of the nation's highest scientific and medical resources—when an unmanned research satellite returns to earth lethally contaminated.

Four American scientists, chosen in advance for their experimental achievements, are summoned under conditions of total news blackout to Wildfire's secret laboratory five stories beneath the Nevada desert. There they work against the threat of a worldwide epidemic to find an antidote to the unknown microorganism that has wiped out all but two inhabitants of a small Arizona town. "Terrifying . . . one of the most important novels of the year."—*Library Journal*

A DELL BOOK $1.25

HOW MANY
OF THESE
<u>NEW</u>
SCIENCE FICTION
STORIES
HAVE YOU
READ?

THE BURNING 95c
by James E. Gunn

DAUGHTERS OF EARTH 75c
by Judith Merril

DIMENSION A 95c
by L. P. Davies

THE POLLINATORS OF EDEN 75c
by John Boyd

THIRTEEN O'CLOCK 75c
by Cecil Corwin

A WILDERNESS OF STARS 95c
William F. Nolan, Editor

If you cannot obtain copies of these titles from your local bookseller, just send the price (plus 15c per copy for handling and postage) to Dell Books, Post Office Box 1000, Pinebrook, N. J. 07058. No postage or handling charge is required on any order of five or more books.